AN
UNLIKELY
HERO

HERO – HERO NOT

M. ESTES

WESTBOW
PRESS
A DIVISION OF THOMAS NELSON

This is a work of fiction. All of the characters, names, incidents,
organizations, and dialogue in this novel are either the products
of the author's imagination or are used fictitiously.

WestBow Press books may be ordered through booksellers or by contacting:

WestBow Press
A Division of Thomas Nelson
1663 Liberty Drive
Bloomington, IN 47403
www.westbowpress.com
1-(866) 928-1240

ISBN: 978-1-4497-3884-6 (sc)
ISBN: 978-1-4497-3883-9 (hc)
ISBN: 978-1-4497-3885-3 (e)

Library of Congress Control Number: 2012901533

Printed in the United States of America

WestBow Press rev. date: 03/07/2012

CONTENTS

ACKNOWLEDGEMENT

Many thanks to George Renshaw, Rick Manning, Karla Downing, Dottie Stewart, and all the other folks who offered words of encouragement, but above all it is with considerable pleasure and pride that I acknowledge the role my wife, Deanna, played in this venture. Without her support and encouragement, I would not have had the vision to start, the patience to spend countless hours engrossed in tedious detail, and the perseverance to see the venture through. Her understanding during periods of frustration fortified me against an ever present temptation to abandon the whole thing. Surely, such support and personal sacrifice by a loving wife is an eloquent statement about the fulfillment on one man's need and, perhaps in a larger sense, a testimony on behalf of the institution of marriage as God intended it to be.

DEDICATION

This story is dedicated to two disparate groups:

First, to people of all ages who live with autism including parents, siblings, grandparents, and others who love and care for those afflicted; and

Second, to all those who resent and resist oppressive, stifling, and thought-controlling political correctness.

CHAPTER 1

On the Scene with Pull Itzer

Pull Itzer, a man of distinction in the news business, sat at his desk in his crowded, office cubicle trying to contain knots of frustration-driven anger in his gut. He had just gotten another story thrown back in his face with a caustic note reminding him that management's agenda must be supported.

Pull responded, "BALONEY," written in bold red ink. "I am not a propagandist. This story accurately reports who, what, when, where, and why. I refuse to change or delete the facts to support the Party line."

"Come on, Pull. You don't get it, my job is on the line, as well as yours. You have got to conform," pleaded his immediate superior. Pull would not capitulate, thus ending his award winning career with the paper that prints "all the news that fits."

Pull adapted quickly to his new role as a freelance reporter/blogger. He loved the independence and had plenty of contacts to make a go of it. Over the years of working for, or with, media giants that monopolized the business, he developed a valuable list of friends "in the know" and did not hesitate to use them.

Returning to his first love of unfettered, investigative reporting, he noticed a provocative story unfolding on the Internet that had not yet been fully, or objectively, covered. It was a story about an autistic kid doing inexplicable things. Since the action had been happening on an elementary school campus in the hometown of an old friend, Captain Jim Studly of the Moreville Police Department, he sent an e-mail inquiring about the truth of the wild stories. Captain Studly's response about the goings-on at Moreville Elementary School intrigued him. The e-mail read, "I don't know what you have read, but we do have a skinny, little kid who seems to be single-handedly decimating the bad guy population hereabouts, much to the chagrin of local ACLA supporters. I have never seen anything like it; he is sort of a hero to his fellow students. You really should check it out."

Pull and Captain Studly, a straight-shooting, straight-talking cop, became close friends when they both worked in Megacity, the big city down the freeway from Moreville. Their friendship was based on mutual respect. Pull knew if Studly said something was true, it was true. Studly's verification that an autistic kid had been doing extraordinary things on a calm, elementary school campus in an upscale neighborhood motivated Pull to drop everything and book a flight west.

Pull Itzer could not have imagined the good fortune that awaited him when he boarded a red-eye flight from the big, East Coast city some called the nation's armpit.

As he entered Moreville, "The Health Food Capital of the World" according to a huge sign on a stylish, glass-covered office building adjacent to the freeway, he got an instant message from his policeman friend. "Another incident involving the kid just occurred at the school. Advise quick response," the message read. He was elated to get this message since he was only minutes away, and soon would be at the scene along with the first responders. "What a break. I really owe Studly for this tip," he thought.

It was a beautiful morning in the land of perpetual spring and summer. "What's not to like about this place?" he mused as he pushed the speed limit while wheeling down the neat, palm tree-lined streets of Moreville in his rental car. He had just gulped down his last swallow of stale coffee after the red-eye flight. Tired but excited, he was running on pure adrenalin. As he pondered what might lie ahead, there it was. He did not have to read the pricy sign on the well-manicured lawn to know he had reached his destination, Moreville Elementary School.

He knew the place would soon look like the media circus he had seen many times before when something unusual happened. He also knew a little aggressive driving would be required to get close to the scene of the incident, which he instinctively knew was in the middle of a rapidly gathering crowd. Grateful for the first time that his rental car was dinky, he skillfully maneuvered it in between an ambulance and a police car as a fire truck and TV broadcast van raced toward the same spot. Jumping from the car with the keys still in the ignition—in case first responders wanted to move it—he entered the schoolyard through a gated fence separating the street from the school. From his vantage point, he could see a hapless-looking man sprawled across the hood of a car parked curbside. On the schoolyard side of the fence was an unassuming-looking kid with gangly legs sitting next to a mother hen-like lady at one of the umbrella covered tables; which reminded him more of a food court in an upscale mall than that of a schoolyard. Judging from the peculiar look on the kid's face and his general demeanor, Pull concluded he was the kid Studly mentioned. "There is something wrong with this picture, that kid looks like the most unlikely hero imaginable," Pull thought. The fence separating the schoolyard from the sidewalk had a smooth hole in it, as if a torpedo had been fired through it. There was no doubt that this was the scene of the incident, and there was also no doubt about who was in charge. Captain Studly moved quickly to bring order to the tense situation, Moreville police personnel cordoned off both sides of the fence including the parked car with the guy on the hood, the entrance gate, and the food court. Reporters and curious by-standers alike rushed about in a frenzy trying to find out what happened.

Pull had an enormous advantage over his competitors because he was already inside the cordoned off "crime scene" area. As a yellow tape-bearing policeman challenged his presence, Captain Studly approached shouting, "Hey, Pull, how did you get here so fast?" Pull's quick wit and good humor flashed through the circumstance, smiling broadly he responded, "You pick up three hours when flying from the armpit to paradise." They both laughed as they warmly greeted each other with a hearty handshake.

Then it was back to business as Pull asked, "Is that kid at the table the 'perp,' as he has been called by some on the Internet? Can I talk to him?"

"Yes, that is the boy. The lady next to him is his teacher, Mary Gonzales; rumor has it she doesn't let any of her kids stray far from sight once they step on campus."

"Sounds like a handy person to have around. Makes your job easier, eh?" Pull responded.

Studly said, "Yep, she is a good gal. You definitely want to talk to her, even though she may not want to talk to you. She does a good job of keeping out of the news."

Studly surveyed the entire area as he talked. "Hang on for a minute, Pull, I'm going to do a quick briefing for the press to set the ground rules. By the way, the only thing I can say is good luck; the boy is not much of a talker." A sly grin overcame his face, "Whatever you do, don't tick him off."

"Hey, come on Studly, how could I tick him off? And what could he do?"

"Look Pull," Studly responded. "I don't know what ticks him off, and you don't personally want to know what he can do. That much I know."

Seeing Pull in what appeared to be a private conversation with Studly, other reporters and information seekers grew impatient—and perhaps jealous. The more aggressive ones attempted to slip under the yellow tape only to be stopped cold by a cadre of heavy-duty Moreville police.

The captain—standing in front of the gathering crowd like a giant in full uniform, was comforting to ordinary citizens but intimidating to bad guys and members of the Americans for Criminal Legal Assistance (ACLA)—stated in a firm but calm voice, "Listen up, people, I have a brief statement to make. This, as you all know, is a crime scene. Do not attempt to enter the cordoned off area."

"It's not fair. That guy is a reporter," a person with a shrill voice interrupted while pointing frantically at Pull.

Studly scanned the crowd until his eyes locked onto the glassy eyes of the person, Nancy Malaprop of *The Megacity Times*, he knew to be the protestor before continuing.

"A crime has been committed here today. The person believed to be the perpetrator of the crime was apprehended by a student at this school. I do not have all the facts at the present. Our report will be available at the conclusion of the investigation. Here is what I know: a young girl, a student of this school in the special education program, was accosted on the sidewalk as she attempted to find her way to the entrance gate. I have been told she may have been disorientated and confused by the new fence and the location of the gate. She apparently lingered on the sidewalk after getting out of her mother's car long enough to attract the attention of a lurking deviant. She has been examined and is in the nurse's office waiting for her parents. Do not disturb the girl. No, I will not reveal her name or the name of the student who allegedly came to her rescue. The girl was heard screaming loudly by a fellow student in the special education program who somehow penetrated the chain-link fence and caused the guy who was trying to nab the little girl to land up on the hood of his car. The student then led the girl by the hand through the gate to their teacher. Note that I said 'allegedly,' as no one has positively identified the male student as the person who actually penetrated the fence and confronted the deviant."

"Would the male student be Criss Cross, the kid who has been in trouble here at this school before?" Nancy Malaprop yelled.

"You have all heard about unusual incidents that occurred here on this campus recently involving a male student in the special education program," Studly said. "There has been considerable press coverage and our reports are a matter of public record. I cannot confirm that this is the same student and, as I said at the outset, I will not reveal his name. Most reporters acknowledge it is not customary to reveal the name of a minor in situations like this. Both students will remain on campus until their respective parents arrive, at which time Moreville Police Department personnel will escort each family to their home."

Studly continued, "I know the public has an interest in being informed, and I know that you folks have a job to do. I also know that both students involved in this incident, the victim and the rescuer, are entitled to protection from possible abuse, badgering, and intimidation. To satisfy and protect all interests, I have selected one among you to talk—I did not say interview—to the young, male student. Pull Itzer, a reporter widely acknowledged for his personal integrity and high ethical standards, will function in that capacity. He will do so with the proviso that his observations and discussions be pooled for mutual access."

Assuming a firm posture reminiscent of his days as a defensive end at Downtown Megacity University (DMU), Studly concluded his remarks with a tone of finality. "The principal of this school usually has comments for the press; I suggest you contact him. That is all."

"Well, where is the principal?" shouted a frantic person in the crowd. Before Studly could respond, an attractive, young lady spoke up, "I am Mr. Noe Itall's assistant. He is not usually available this early in the day, but my assistant is preparing a statement for Mr. Noe Itall's review as we speak." Pull made a note to himself, "The principal, who doesn't get here at the opening bell, has an assistant who has an assistant to do press releases; the kid isn't the only thing strange about this school."

As Studly spoke to the crowd of reporters, Pull listened intently. His focus, however, was on the boy at the table. The boy gave a shoulder-shrugging, face-contorting flinch as two shrill blurps came from the emergency ambulance as it gently maneuvered through the crowd—presumably with the alleged child attacker, under police guard, on board.

Pull huddled briefly with his media colleagues to work out details of pooling the information he expected to gain during his talk with the boy and his teacher before moving quickly toward the table. He was equipped only with Studly's briefing and experience gained from other difficult interviews. Relying on his big, friendly smile and calm demeanor—which worked so well throughout his career—he courteously approached the teacher with an outstretched hand and requested permission to talk to her student. The emergency ambulance let out another shrill blurp-blurp at a nearby intersection, causing the boy to squirm while loudly asking his teacher, "Why don't they fix that thing, and what are all these people doing here?"

Pull then dropped to one knee and extended his hand to the frail-looking, blond-haired boy with a crooked smile and one eye slightly closed as if trying to avoid the sun, and said, "Hello, my name is Pull Itzer, what is yours?" Pull was impressed that the boy greeted him with a firm handshake and a faint smile while making eye contact for a fleeting second. While the eye contact was brief, it was penetrating. Pull turned away slightly and said to Mary Gonzales, "Wow, I felt like the boy just looked right through me."

Gonzales, flashing a friendly "got you" kind of grin, lightened the tension that was in the air as she said, "Some people are easy to see through." The unexpected response caused Pull to burst into spontaneous laughter.

The boy answered Pull's question. "My name is Criss Crosswauld," he said while looking down at a medal he was clutching in both hands.

Just then, two emergency medical technicians hurriedly appeared with a stretcher. The lead technician said, "Sorry to interrupt, even though we have already examined this young man, we have been ordered to make absolutely certain he is not injured. So, we are going to take another look, especially at his feet and legs. It won't take long. We have already given him every field test available, and he is in excellent condition, not a scratch on him. They seem to want us to take him to emergency as a precaution, but there is no way I could justify exposing this kid to an unnecessary trauma-inducing ride in an ambulance."

The second technician, a young lady, squatted down beside Criss and attempted to engage him in light conversation saying, "My, that is a pretty medal you have. Where did you get it?"

Criss haltingly said, "Uh, uh—my, my uncle."

The lead technician said, "Hey, can I see that medal? It looks like the Navy Cross." Criss, with his head turned slightly so that he faced no one straight on, replied with a tone bordering on defiance, "No, no. I won't give it to anyone."

Mary Gonzales moved quickly to Criss's side. With a hand on his shoulder she said, "Please understand Criss is not being rude. He, like others with neurological challenges, communicates on a different level. Don't you think that is enough questioning?"

As he prepared to depart in the remaining ambulance meant for Criss, the lead technician said, "Yes, ma'am. Sorry, I got carried away. I spent four years as a Corpsman, and this is the closest I ever came to a Navy Cross. Whoever earned that medal is one brave dude; they don't give many of them out. You gotta wonder how the kid got it."

Pull noted that Mary Gonzales was firm but tactful. He immediately liked her style and attempted to arrange a more in-depth interview. She became aloof and reluctant to speak to anyone who acted like a reporter giving him the impression that she just might have something to hide. He also noted that there had to be a story behind that medal.

Pull then resumed his position of kneeling on one knee in front of Criss, hoping to make more eye contact, "Criss, some people say you made that big hole in the fence. Did you do that?"

Criss said, "Uh, um, I dunno; I guess. Am I in trouble? My mom doesn't like it when I break things."

Pull then asked, "How did you know your friend needed your help?"

"Ah, well, she called me."

"Did she call your name?"

"Ah, I think so. Ah, ah, I dunno."

Pull then asked, "Where were you when she called?"

Criss said, "Oh—ah—I was going to Miss Mary's class over there," as he pointed without looking toward the special education area about one hundred yards away.

Someone yelled, "They are here." Pull was surprised by a sudden mood change in the crowd. It went from a noisy, milling around scene to near silence as Criss's anxious family arrived being accompanied by two Moreville police officers.

The crowd formed a neat, tight line along the yellow tape defining the "crime scene," which was tight enough to force pushy reporters and camera crews to keep their distance. Capt. Studly quickly stepped forward to greet the parents. He immediately escorted the family to the area where Criss and Mary Gonzales were waiting.

The sight was astonishing as Criss reached out to high five his brother and embrace his mom and dad. The crowd broke into loud applause and shouts of praise for Criss.

Capt. Studly and his band of patrolmen escorted the family away from the site as students wearing odd-looking T-shirts broke into the still tightly formed line to offer Criss energetic high fives of their own. Pull noted that it was impressive how parents and other onlookers allowed students to slip seamlessly to the front of the line next to the yellow tape. Then, Pull got a good look at those odd T-shirts which were emblazoned with a symbol of twisted electrical wires and slogans that read things like "CROSS WIRE SAVES." This, like everything else around Moreville Elementary, pushed the limits of believability. The kid had a fan club. This unlikely specimen of humanity was a hero. No! He was a superhero.

Studly, lagging behind the police who were escorting Criss and his family, turned to Pull and said, "I will fill you in on the other incidents that have happened on this campus later. How about dinner this evening? Alice will be expecting you to drop by, you know."

Pull said, "Terrific, I would love seeing your family again. I am looking forward to seeing them and excited to learn more about your little hero."

Pull knew this story would have real legs as it broke, and he was fortunate to be on site. He would have to hustle to get this on his Web site fast. He stood there in the crowded line peering over the cheering kids. He quickly posted highlights of his first encounter with Criss Cross—the superhero—on his hot, new hand-held, do-everything phone. It went to his Web site, as well as news outlets affiliated with the syndicate to which he belonged. He could not help but silently thank God for the new tech stuff; it made real-time reporting possible.

Pull knew that in the crazy world of the news biz, this would cause him to be looked upon as the authority on Criss Cross. All this before his competitors could run with the story. By the time the skilled news crews were featured on the nightly news and the printing presses rolled with their stories, they would only confirm what he had already reported in real-time. The thought of all this caused Pull to mutter to himself, "I am glad I was on top of this story first. Maybe my reporting will motivate some of those slaves-to-political-correctness guys to keep their stories straight. I don't see any racial component to this story at all, as implied in the *Megacity Times* stories about previous incidents."

As the excitement subsided, Pull remained pumped-up as he outlined, in his mind, what he needed to do to tell this intriguing story and get to the bottom of the mystery surrounding Moreville's unusual hero. Eager to stick with the story until all leads had been explored, Pull began a quest for answers to what made Criss Cross tick. Captivated by the uniqueness of the situation, he persuaded his sponsors to cover expenses of doing this story "right" from one end to the other.

Thus began an amazing journalistic venture into a complex and little understood world. Pull knew chasing this story would be difficult, but he had absolutely no inkling of the surprises and even shock awaiting him. He was ill prepared for what he was getting into, but excitement and intrigue was what he missed in his old "tow-the-party-line" job. The behavior of this little guy, with a Pervasive Developmental Disorder (PDD), would change Pull's life. It seemed logical to start by studying police reports, published articles, and broadcast transcripts. He also wanted to investigate, where available, personal diaries and e-messages from people around the world that discussed "Cross Wire the Mysterious" as a popular, local TV news personality called Criss. Pull already had the medal angle and the aloofness of Mary Gonzales to work with, and he knew there would be many other hunches and leads to follow. But first, he had to bone up on the thing that made Criss unique, aside from his exploits and medical condition. "What is this thing called PDD?" he wondered. He knew that no matter how much research he did, this story, more than any other he had done before, would be a challenge.

As Pull sat down at the simple, yet elegant, dinner table at the Studly home that evening memories of his wife gushed to the surface of his conscious thoughts like a geyser. She was gone now, the victim of a sudden, virulent illness. Alice Studly, gracious and caring, reminded him of her. It was distracting, and he had to admit to himself that he was a little envious of his old buddy, Jim Studly.

The dinner was social, but as is often the case when two professionals with a common interest get together in a relaxing atmosphere, the subject got around to business; in this case, Criss Crosswauld. After all, Studly did promise to fill him in on what had been going on.

Studly told Pull what he knew about the kid's exploits, saying, "Criss's name was changed by a local reporter, Nancy Malaprop, from Criss Crosswauld to Criss Cross as she reported on his punching out the school bully. The new moniker stuck like a lot of stuff that is abbreviated sticks these days. Malaprop took a lot of heat for revealing his name even if it was the wrong name, not to mention the speculation that she wanted to slur him because she reported Criss's first conflict as if it was a hate crime perpetrated on a minority."

Pull said, "Unprofessional reporting like that is one of my pet peeves. If the kid's parents object to made-up names, I absolutely will not use them no matter how catchy they can be. By the way, I caught that hate crime angle on the Internet and in the local newspaper accounts. Isn't the school bully a big kid?"

"Yes. I'd say the bully is at least twice Criss's size, but I have to admit I really don't know much about Criss himself. My guys have been out to the Crosswauld home a few times which has generated a lot of talk at the station, but the whole situation surrounding the family is a bit of a mystery," Studly said.

"Hey, I have gotta poke at that mystery stuff; you know me, I love a mystery," Pull said with his usual grin that made him a hard man to read.

"Talking about mysteries," Pull said, "what is with that huge sign I saw coming into town proclaiming Moreville to be the health food capital?"

"Oh!" Studly said, "That must be the Allypoop Technology headquarters building you saw. It is a big, international company founded by the city's namesake James B. More. I guess they sell a lot of vitamins."

Pull said, "Um vitamins, superhero, anyone ever try to tie that together?"

"I don't know, never connected the two myself. But I have a feeling you just might look into that possibility, um Pull."

Studly went on to say, "This incident today was the most dramatic but just the latest of several similar incidents that have happened on the campus recently. Every incident resulted in a police report being compiled, they are all public records. Come on down and help yourself. After a long reflective pause, Studly continued, "After all these years, I am sort of hardened. I've seen a lot of strange things, but there is nothing that I've seen or heard of that compares to what has been going on. This kid has attracted bad guys like a magnet attracts metal filings. Playground bullies and common criminals alike have now felt his wrath."

"As an officer of the law, I am troubled because it is always the same. My guys take statements from witnesses or near witnesses at each incident, including today's. I know they are not truthful witnesses when they claim it happens so fast that they cannot positively identify Criss as the person involved, and I don't know how to handle it. On the one hand, dishonesty at any level bothers me; on the other hand, I am relieved because I personally identify with the kid. 'I didn't see it clearly,' has become the standard response from eyeball witnesses; they are afraid the kid will get in trouble if they I.D. him. A vociferous group says I should press witnesses harder. I hope and pray I am not forced to take a harder line at some point down the road."

Studly explained that his dilemma was unlike any he had ever had in his career. "Today I wanted to praise the kid publicly, and thank him for taking the low-life criminal off the streets. He deserves praise as much as anyone I have ever met; he may very well have saved the girl's life. But I know full well that the Americans for Criminal Legal Assistance (ACLA) crowd would make a lot of trouble for the police department and the whole darn town if I did that. They have already labeled the kid a ruthless vigilante and demanded that he be locked up like an insane person in an asylum. So, I just discreetly gave him a little slap on the back, gave his dad a supportive handshake, and wished them well as they went home. It tears at me that so many of our politically powerful citizens won't tolerate actions or statements that don't conform to their worldview."

Pull said, "I know what you mean. We seem to be caught up in a nationwide pandemic of downward-spiraling, public morality."

After a little small talk about kids and sports, Pull skillfully directed the conversation where he wanted it to go. "As I was looking over the Moreville city map to find your home, I noticed that the address for the Adam and Evelyn Crosswauld family is nearby. Do you happen to know them?"

Jim responded, "No. But as I said, my guys have visited their home on a few occasions. I feel like I know them; but I really don't. They are sort of new in town, as are we, and it takes a little time to get established here in Moreville."

Alice joined the conversation, interjecting, "Evelyn Crosswauld, or Eve as everyone seems to call her, is in the PTA with me. I see her shopping and have casual chats with her. I have often thought it would be neighborly to invite them over for dinner, but with Jim's job it is kind of hard to be as friendly as we would like. You can imagine what the ACLA crowd, especially Hillary Cheatalot, would do if they thought the police captain met socially with the Crosswauld family. They seem to hate the Crosswaulds so much. Perhaps it is because of the trouble Hillary Cheatalot had with Eve at a PTA meeting."

Pull said, "Wait a minute, Alice. Who the heck is Hillary Cheatalot?"

Alice said, "Oh, that' right, you have been out of the area for a long time so you wouldn't know Cheatalot. She is an influential attorney who is very well connected politically. I think everyone in town knows her, or knows about her."

"Well, that sounds like another item to look into."

"By the way Alice, you mentioned inviting the Crosswaulds to dinner. If you could arrange such a dinner, I would be very grateful to be invited. And I promise to behave like the gentleman you would like me to be." Pull responded with a mischievous grin.

After hearty laughs all around, Alice came right back, "Hey, Pull, I'll do my best to line something up, and if I do, I might just announce it at the next PTA meeting. Hillary will find out anyway," again prompting good-natured laughs all around.

CHAPTER 2

About Criss

Arriving early at the home of Jim and Alice Studly with drinks for the evening, Pull said, "Alice, you said in your invitation that the dinner would be Mediterranean, so I brought some wine. But I think you know I didn't have a clue about what would be appropriate. I hope I didn't mess up, I relied on the clerk at Bennie's Deli down the street from my extended-stay hotel to advise me on the proper dinner and after dinner wine as I wondered, 'What's the difference?'"

Alice gave him a compassionate smile and said, "You really miss her don't you?"

"Yes, I do. I miss her every day, but at times like this it is really hard. I just don't do social things; that was her specialty."

"Don't worry about a thing, rest assured that in this house you can't make a mistake."

"Thanks for understanding Alice, I just hope the Crosswaulds are not the fussy wine sipper, cork-smelling types."

Alice answered in her usual reassuring manner, "I don't know them well, but I am sure we will find them to be regular folks just like us. I am looking forward to getting to know them as much as you are. Thanks for prodding me into inviting them over. I should have done it a long time ago."

The phone rang just then causing Alice to become a little upset, saying to the caller, "Of course I want to see you before you leave. You know that. It is just that we have guests coming for dinner, and I don't know if I can work it in. Let me get right back to you."

The caller was a friend from college who was in town and only had that evening free. Alice desperately wanted to see her old friend, as they were very close. Telling Jim and Pull of her predicament, they both heartily agreed that she should just tell her friend to come over.

"The more the merrier, as the saying goes," Jim said.

Jim knew Alice's friend. The girls were friends when they all attended Downtown Megacity University (DMU) several years back. He thought to himself, "She was a real looker in those days, and I think she is single. This could be Pull's lucky day."

The doorbell rang, causing Alice to exclaim, "Oh no! They are here, and I am not nearly ready."

Alice heard Jim say, "Well hello, Agatha. What a pleasant surprise. Come on in."

"Hey, come on Jim, remember me? I am still just Aggie." After a cordial exchange of greetings, Alice introduced Aggie to Pull and quickly went back to her preparations for dinner as Aggie eagerly pitched in to help.

Alice turned to Aggie in a casual way and asked, "Have you met Pull before? I got the feeling that you knew him."

"Oh no, don't know the guy. The name is familiar. I have probably seen his by-line on a news story or something. Is Pull his real name?"

"I don't know; he has always been Pull the news guy. Our kids thought he was the guy who delivered the morning newspaper," she said laughingly. "I'll ask him about his funny name. It might make for good conversation."

The two guys adjourned to the den, but not before Jim suggested that, since Pull brought the good wine for dinner and after dinner, perhaps a glass of merlot would be in order; as he whipped out a bottle of Cheap Chuck's best.

The conversations were light and breezy in the kitchen as well as the den, catching up on old times. The party was off to a good start.

Then, right at the scheduled time, the doorbell rang again. Jim, based on his prior observations, expected the Crosswaulds to be on time, plus or minus a minute or so. Again, introductions all around, another glass of Cheap Chuck's for the guys and who knew what for the gals. The women seemed to be unusually comfortable with each other, laughing and tee-heeing like high school kids as they prepared dinner.

The dinner was incredible, and Pull said so. Eve added, "And the wine was an excellent choice as well." She could not have known how much that little comment meant to Pull.

As the three couples seated themselves in the Studly's comfortable den, a warm glow from the fireplace added to the friendly ambiance. Jim broke out Pull's after dinner wine. As he did he thought, "I would never have bought this stuff. I can't even pronounce it."

It seemed that everyone wanted to talk and get acquainted or reacquainted. There was an air of openness that, even among old friends, was seldom seen.

Alice, in her engaging, friendly manner sought an answer to Aggie's question. "Hey Pull, I have been wondering where you got your interesting name."

To which Pull responded, grinning broadly, "You're not the only one that has asked that question. It is very simple really. My last name came from my dad, a Jewish boy who married a Catholic girl who was devoted to St. Paul, so I became Paul Itzer. I remained Paul Itzer until a smart-mouth kid in my high school journalism class started calling me Pull. Nicknames have a way of sticking sometimes."

Adam said, "We know all about nicknames sticking, our boy Criss has one. But he doesn't care so we don't worry about it. We just take it in stride. It is really all we can do."

Pull interjected, "So, you don't mind your boy being called Criss Cross in the press?"

"We don't really mind, but it was callous and cruel of the *Megacity Times* reporter to arbitrarily rename our boy; and we told her so. But she didn't seem to care what we thought," said Eve.

Adam then asked in a lighthearted way if it was true that at least fifty percent of the people present went to DMU?

"Not I," quipped Pull. "I went to that other football college, you know, where they wear golden helmets."

Adam laughingly responded, "Well, that seems to be about the only thing they teach at DMU, right, Jim?"

Jim shot back with a big laugh, "Come on, Adam. That is a little harsh. They also teach baseball and basketball. Talking about football, the name Crosswauld rings a bell. Did you play the game, Adam?"

"Yeah," Adam responded. "I made the team at a different school than my brother, but I never played at his level; he was outstanding. You must be thinking about him."

"Would that be Jocko Crosswauld, the All-American Q-back at the Academy?" Jim asked.

Jim continued, "We never played the Academy at DMU, so I never saw him play. But he was an impressive player with class, that's for sure."

"Yep, Jocko was an extraordinary person in every respect," Adam responded.

"Whatever happened to Jocko? I have not heard anything about him in years?" Pull inquired.

"You know, I really don't want to get into all that; call it sibling rivalry if you like," came the subdued response from Adam.

A little more lighthearted chitchat followed. Then Adam, knowing that everyone was curious about Criss, said casually, "Well, I'll bet you folks would like to know about our boy, Criss. Everyone seems to be curious about him."

Eve quickly added, "I want you to know that he is not the crazed maniac some have called him on the Internet. He is the most gentle, loving child you would ever want to meet. We don't know what gets into him at times, but we have never had a discipline problem with him. And he has never, ever hurt an innocent person."

Adam continued, "He was a little unusual right from the very first day we brought him home from the hospital. He has been receiving medical attention and medication his whole life. I suppose under any circumstance he would have been considered unusual, but many things seemed to converge in his young life to make him what he is today. As you all know, his feats have propelled him to rock star like status here in Moreville."

"Yes," Eve said. "And we don't know how to handle it. As you might image his behavior is causing a few problems, but we are proud of him for standing up for what is right. And, no, we don't have a clue how he does what he does, but we have a pretty good idea why he does it. He just plain does not like injustice; he wants everyone to be fair."

Adam continued, "We are expanding our home to accommodate my mom, and I have been meaning to talk to someone at City Hall about a stranger who showed up, claiming to be a security expert. He persuaded us to drop the idea of building a self-contained cottage for mom and to bump out a few walls instead, so that everything would be under one roof. He also gave us advice on security sensors. Do you know anything about that, Jim?"

Pull made a mental note that Aggie seemed to flinch at that question. He found her easy to look at and was not sure that his keen interest was as dispassionate as the reporter inside of him felt it should be.

Jim claimed to know nothing about the security guy.

With a slight trace of sarcasm, Adam went on to say, "I went to the public college; West Side Megacity University (WSMU), not the other place." It was clear that he was throwing in a little good-natured dig at his newly found DMU alumni friends. "But I still picked up a desire to keep up with the Joneses. If I can just find a Jones family in town with a bump-out, I'll be Ok," he said with a self-depreciating laugh.

Adam went on to relate what it was like having a boy with a developmental disorder. "Criss sort of put a cramp on our social plans for awhile because we did not know how he would interact with other families. It has been a learning experience. Thankfully, much of our anxiety was unfounded. At times, things get a little awkward, but it is a small price to pay for having such a loving kid in the family. I was disturbed and scared by my own thoughts of what life would hold for Criss. Recent events have magnified my fears which are shared by Eve and, to a lesser extent, his brother Jack."

Adam continued, "Criss was a scrawny little tow-headed kid, small for his age and totally uncoordinated. He was late with potty training and learning basic skills like tying his shoelaces. The whole family tried to get him to play catch or do any number of tasks to develop his motor skills. Criss just did not seem to understand the point of it all. We never knew if he did not do simple tasks because he could not, or if he did not do them because he would not. He preferred the solitude of his own company, which could become loud and a little blusterous. Criss could do one physical activity really well; he could run far and fast. But he didn't seem to know when to run."

Adam went on to say, "We have all tried to conceal our feelings about the awkwardness of Criss's behavior. I struggled with the thought that I would never enjoy the vicarious experience of watching Criss excel, if only for a few moments, at something—anything. But his brother Jack does well at many things, creating a dilemma. How can a dad in a situation like this show pride in the accomplishments of one son without inadvertently making the other feel inferior? In a sense, it has probably been a little like my dad felt raising me in my big brother's shadow."

"Eve, at least on the surface, never has let the prospect of raising a handicapped child depress her. She has taken a pragmatic view that things are what they are, and we just have to make the best of it. She has kept very busy taking the boys here and there, with little time for asking, 'why me?' or otherwise letting her anxiety flair up openly. She has been a great mom," Adam said.

Pull said, "I have heard about autism, and I am beginning to do a literature search in hopes of being authentic in my commentaries. Can you share what it is like in your family?"

"Sure, I like talking about our boy. We do all the things other families do. In some ways it is very interesting, and I am not talking about the incidents that happened at Moreville Elementary. What I mean is he can be surprisingly talented and entertaining at times, and he is almost always upbeat and happy."

Adam went on to say, "Criss, like some other autistic children, has remarkable skills in certain narrowly focused areas. For instance, Criss loves books and reads above his grade level; pronouncing each word with a phonetic precision that would match that of a kid educated at a stiff and proper British school. We don't know how much he comprehends, but he knows a lot of interesting stuff that tumbles out at unexpected times."

Alice asked, "Do you think he has a photographic memory?"

Eve responded, "Well, we aren't sure about that but like Adam said, he comes up with some awesome stuff. His memory for certain details is, at times, exceptional. It is not uncommon for him to memorize the entire script of a favorite character in a TV show."

Adam added, "These are good things in my eyes because it seems to leave the door open that maybe, just maybe, Criss will be some kind of a late bloomer; perhaps a genius of some kind. Nothing he has done gave us a hint that he had any latent strength or potential to do the supernatural-like things he has done recently."

"God only knows what is going on that enables him to perform these feats, they are way out of character for him. Maybe my thoughts and prayers were prophetic; they could be acts of a genius redefined," Adam said smiling once again showing his low-key sense of humor.

Eve added, "He is an easy kid to love. We have done all that we know to do. He has the best professional help available, but we have found that the experts don't agree among themselves. We have tried the lactose, gluten, casein-free diet as suggested, thinking there might be an allergy related problem. We have tried just about everything that seemed to hold any hope, but nothing has worked. We have finally settled into a common-sense approach with a balanced diet, a child-size multi-vitamin, and minimum medication. Of course, we are keen on physical fitness, but that was really hard to regulate until we finally realized his natural love for running provided plenty of exercise. We do not even have to encourage it; he just does it."

Adam said, "One thing all the professionals agreed on was that Moreville Elementary is best equipped to handle the special needs of Criss, given its new emphasis on special education. This new program, which integrated the two accepted early intervention approaches—behavior and developmental—seemed promising. It was the reason we sacrificed to buy a home we could barely afford here in Moreville. We admit that a Moreville zip code did not hurt our mutual notion of being upwardly mobile; but you can be sure, that was the least of our concerns. We just wanted to help our boy."

Jim asked, "Did you folks get him involved in sports? One would think that if he had latent energy and strength it would have been evident in sports."

Adam said, "That's a reasonable expectation, but it didn't happen."

"We had a common awareness in our family that growing up could be a difficult struggle for Criss, if he did not develop some social skills and an interest in the things other kids do. Hoping against hope that he would grow out of his awkwardness, we signed him up for the usual childhood sports: soccer, tennis, judo, and anything else we could think of. We tried desperately to find something that would interest him. By the way, Hillary Cheatalot, the big-time attorney who lives locally, has been heard saying that it might have been the six weeks of judo training that turned Criss into the monster he is. Can you believe that?" This caused an outburst of laughter and head shaking on the part of his new friends.

Adam went on to explain that soccer was the most trying experience. "Criss could not do much more than nudge the ball down the field at best, and he never knew which direction the ball was supposed to go."

Eve quickly added, "It was sort of funny in a way. The soccer coach put Criss in games as goalie to please Adam here. On the rare occasions when the opposing teams of seven and eight-year-olds did kick the ball toward the goal, Criss had no idea what to do. He would let the ball sail right by, often without even looking at it. On a good attempt at blocking the kick, he would wave in the direction of the ball. The coach was kind and understood that every kid deserved a chance to develop. But enough was enough; the other kids complained, the parents complained, and Criss was not very happy either."

Eve shrugged her shoulders indicating her acceptance. "The coach made the very difficult decision to tell Adam, whom you may have noticed is a competitive guy in his own right, that it just was not fair to the other team members to play Criss at any position. Adam knew the coach was right and accepted the reality of the situation gracefully, but that did not make it any easier. Criss's soccer career ended before it began, much to the sorrow of everyone involved, except Criss."

Adam went on to say, "He did not seem to mind at all. He never liked it anyway because the other kids were always shouting at him and calling him names. Criss became more and more socially isolated, playing solitaire games, sometimes under a table, with cars or plastic army men. He seemed content making odd, often loud, noises as he played by the hour making up his own rules in his own private world; in his own reality."

When asked how the family was holding up, Adam responded, "We are a very close family, and we have support from families in our church. Somehow we will get through all this confusion." As his voice trailed off, he said almost in a whisper, "If it weren't for those darn, harassing letters threatening lawsuits, we could breathe a lot easier."

Jim blurted out loudly, "What! Don't tell me they are going to sue you for what Criss has done in his own defense and in defense of others? Why doesn't that surprise me?"

"It sure looks like it. I think Hillary Cheatalot is representing everyone Criss has had a beef with. She calls them the 'twelve victims of Criss Cross.' She doesn't even use his real name."

Pull exclaimed, "Hey that just doesn't seem right! Have you thought of trying to get some legal help, pro bono?"

"Well, no, I am not even sure what that means. Does that mean free? I would not know how to go about something like that," Adam said shaking his head with a puzzled look on his face.

At that point, Aggie broke her long period of silence saying, "I know an expert in setting up 501(c) non-profit foundations who would very likely be willing to get involved. I think I can speak for him in this matter. He is an old friend from DMU and does pro bono work from time to time. Pull, you could be the catalyst and get this thing launched overnight with your blog; after all, you are considered to be the authority on all things Criss related, are you not?"

Pull was taken aback by the boldness of this gal. She darn well knew a lot more about this Criss phenomenon thing than she previously let on. "Umm, what is going on here?" Pull thought. He collected his wits with a lingering sense of self-doubt and a little inner voice reminding him that reporters don't get emotionally carried away.

Pull said, "Darn right, I can help. But I have got to tell you all that I know zilch about record keeping and that sort of thing."

"Not to worry, that base is easy to cover. So are we all agreed? Let's get the Criss Cross Defense Fund launched ASAP," Aggie said with firm resolution. Then, turning to Adam and Eve with a look of pride and resolve, she asked, "What do you guys think?"

The young couple, sitting side-by-side on the big, comfortable couch, instantly reached for each other's hand as Eve, fighting back tears, said, "We don't know what to say! We are overwhelmed by your sincere interest in our problems. Thank you—thank you all."

With that, the little party broke up and everyone headed for the front door. The ladies were smiling and embracing while the men shook hands and slapped each other on the back.

Pull wanted to pin that Aggie babe down. He had to find out how she knew so much, and how she just happened to show up at the right time. "Some coincidence," he thought.

Aggie disappeared as he paused for one last word with Jim. Pull thought he saw her drive off rapidly in a mid-sized car that had the look of a government issued vehicle.

Had Pull been in the car with Aggie, he would have heard one side of a coded phone message that said, "Contact made; too early to calibrate all players. Schedule satisfied thus far."

CHAPTER 3

Criss's Defense Team

Pull's repeated comments about the "Defend Criss Fund" on his Web site and print commentaries brought a deluge of responses. Just as Aggie had predicted, Slip Knott, the nerdy lawyer she claimed to know from college, had the legal work finished. The legal formalities were completed so fast, Pull wondered if it weren't done before it was requested. His skeptical nature kicked into high gear as he made a mental note to get this matter resolved. He knew Aggie had the answer. Pull began to wonder what he had gotten himself into as the circumstances surrounding this strong-willed lady became ever stranger.

Jimmie More and his mother, Mrs. James B. More, persuaded James B. (Bigbucks) More Jr. to sponsor a gala fundraising event. It would be held at the More mansion naturally. The "big man" was more than pleased to get involved because he thought it was a good cause, and he had a slightly less noble motivation. The price for attending the event was set at a modest $1,000. Invitations went out to all the "in-people" on list A, and to all those who wanted to be "in-people" on list B.

As Eve went over the list of those responding, she was both amused and perplexed when she saw that Hillary Cheatalot had responded and might very well attend the fundraising event. She sighed softly, to no one in particular, "This must be what they mean when talking about the price of admission to the right social circles. Such irony, the very person who has all but declared war on my family has contributed to the family's legal defense fund. It is harder for me to understand such hypocrisy than it is to understand what makes Criss tick. I will endure this madness and whatever else may come along for Criss's sake, but I don't like it one bit."

The party was hugely successful; great food, good music, and special entertainment, as was always the case when Mrs. James B. More hosted a party. Everyone who was anyone knew she loved planning and being the hostess. It gave her something to do.

Mary Gonzales, Ph.D., the specialist on neurological disorders and the head of Special Education at Moreville Elementary School, gave a brief but informative presentation on Criss's disorder to fill the time as the band took a leisurely break. There was never a dull moment at a Mrs. James B. More party.

This get-together was a great opportunity for Mr. James B. More Jr., or James B. as his friends called him, to do something he had been thinking about since Criss first made the news. Always the businessman, he asked Adam to join him in the library for a brandy. "Just call me James B.," he told Adam. "It makes the conversation much less formal and helps build good relationships."

"Wow!" Adam thought. "What's this all about?"

James B. verbally danced around with Adam before driving to his objective. James B. was skilled. A little football talk and other incidental stuff, before he led into the often-told story of how his father had founded Alleypoop Technology. "My father was an adventuresome, young chemist who went off to the South Pacific in search of a legendary plant that, when properly compounded and applied by a shaman, enhanced native tribesmen's strength and longevity. After several years of searching, he finally found the plant. With the help of a famous botanist and a small team of scientists, the active ingredients in the rare plant natives called Alipop—which sounded like Alleypoop—were synthesized and ready for the market he had already created. He was also a very good businessman."

"You see, Adam," James B. went on in a more serious vein, "Alleypoop Technology, as I am sure you know, is a very big enterprise committed to discovering new and better health products. You can be a part of our future, Adam. What we would like to do is have exclusive rights to whatever findings we come up with when we examine Criss."

"Wait! What do you mean 'examine Criss?'"

"Oh, we would give Criss a complete physical, you might say, in our world-class lab to ascertain what his body chemistry is. It would not be harmful to Criss and actually could become very lucrative for the Crosswauld family. What do you think?"

Adam hid his anger as he responded like an interested businessman instead of the loving, protective father and said, "I don't know what to think. Others have made similar inquiries. I'll have to get back to you, Mr. More, ah, James B."

"I understand. Take your time, Adam, but let me give you something to think about in the meantime. Criss is a phenomenon. Phenomenal people sell products, which, in turn, cause other people to work in making the products. That is what keeps the economy going. Advertisers wanting to associate Criss with everything from shoes to vitamins probably will approach you. APT Inc. rarely uses personal endorsements, but Criss just might be the exception. If you give him a child's multi-vitamin, which I suspect you do, he probably is taking our product already. Why not cash in on it?"

Adam, still a little weary of this high-powered executive, responded the only way he could, "Thanks, Mr. More, uh I mean James B., I'll keep it in mind."

Within a matter of days, money started flowing into the newly established legal defense fund. A hastily formed interim board of directors was set up to manage the fund. Pull accepted a temporary position on the board. It was in this capacity that brought him back to the More mansion shortly after the gala fundraising event.

Pull, even with all his worldliness, was a little intimidated sitting at the huge conference table in the spacious library in the More mansion. He arrived early hoping to talk with Aggie before the other interim members arrived. It was the first time he had been inside the impressive James B. More Jr. mansion, other than the party. He could not help wondering what it would be like to live in a place like this.

He was deeply satisfied that he had been the primary driver in bringing this whole thing about. His timely announcements of the defense fund formation in his blog, and in his nationally syndicated commentary, brought so much money and pledges of money into the Fund, that they were faced with the pleasant thought of what to do with the likely surplus.

Aggie, who suddenly seemed to get transferred from wherever she worked to the Moreville area, was next to arrive, which pleased Pull. She looked terrific. He had a few minutes alone with her, if he could only think of something to say, something polite, clever, and hopefully memorable. Nothing came to mind, so he concluded his best approach would be the usual smile and nod routine.

Within minutes, the hastily formed interim board comprised of Alice Studly, Mary Gonzales, Agatha Etsirhc, Jimmie More, and Pull Itzer arrived. Each reluctantly agreed to fill in as proxies for the official board members, high-powered associates of Mr. James B. More Jr. They did so to keep the momentum going. Also attending the meeting were the legal guy, Slip Knott, Esq. and a recording secretary.

Slip Knott stated, "Thanks largely to Mr. More's influence, the Fund has enough resources to defend the Crosswaulds against any and all legal actions pending or anticipated. The board should also consider what to do with surplus funds if, in fact, there are surplus funds."

The youngest member by far, Jimmie More, an eighth grader, who like others present was attending his first meeting of the Fund's board, was comfortable in this important role; and well prepared. In a strong, confident manner beyond what could reasonably be expected from a boy his age, he said, "Folks, I have read about the neurological condition Criss has, and I believe research in the appropriate fields of science which might lead to a better understanding, and perhaps treatment and a cure, is worthy and appropriate. I, therefore, make a motion that funds deemed to be surplus shall be donated to a legitimate, non-political and non-self-serving entity engaged in such research." A unanimous *second* to Jimmie's motion could have been heard all over the mansion. There was no discussion as the astonished board members voted unanimously to accept the motion.

A few more items of business were discussed, and the meeting was adjourned. Jimmie sat quietly as the board members showered him with compliments for his calm and articulate comments. All agreed this kid was outstanding and would be a great asset to the interim board.

Pull worked his way over to the after-meeting refreshment table where Aggie and Alice were chatting and said, "Aggie, if you don't mind, I would like to ask you a few questions." With that, Alice excused herself and disappeared like a vapor. Pull said, with his trademark smile, "Do you think the Mores would mind if we chatted awhile out on the patio? It looks quiet and inviting."

Aggie said, "Sure," as she thought, 'here it comes.' She sensed Pull was suspicious and becoming impatient for answers. It had to happen eventually.

Bringing their coffee and pastries with them, Pull and Aggie settled into the large, comfortable patio chairs and enjoyed the beautiful view overlooking Moreville, which spread before them like a picture of tranquility and beauty one might find on a postcard. Pull broke the tranquility abruptly, "OK! Aggie, what is going on here? You know a lot more than you let on about this whole situation. You owe me an explanation; otherwise, being a snoopy reporter, I might uncover a couple of facts and get a lot of exercise jumping to conclusions." That softened Pull's purposefully direct question.

"You are right, Pull, I have been avoiding you because I didn't want this conversation until I knew how to handle it. Besides, it would be a shame to see you waste all that energy jumping to conclusions."

"What do you mean, 'how to handle it?' Why not just shoot straight?" Pull exclaimed with an alarming degree of sternness.

"Have you got your recorder? If so, turn the darn thing off and keep it off. Anything I tell you is confidential. Got that, Pull? Confidential!" she replied.

"I would like to lay everything out for you, but I just can't. We are dealing with some sensitive stuff here. We had to do a more thorough background check on you, part of which was my personal observation, before you were cleared for security. Your appearance on the scene was cause for considerable concern until we got you calibrated."

"Oh, I know you had a high-level security clearance when you were flying those jungle missions years ago. My job has been to verify that you are not currently involved in any activities that would, in any way, put your integrity and loyalty in question. The Agency had to be sure that you place national security above the public's right to know. My boss is fully aware that any reporter would be tempted to leak the story I am about to tell you. You see, Pull, the Agency is gambling that you are strong enough to resist the temptation to make a big name for yourself. You now have what is called a 'Necessity Clearance.' Please understand that there are not many in your profession, or any other profession, who would be granted such a clearance."

"Aggie, what in the world are you talking about?"

"Look, Pull, this thing is about Jack, or Jocko Crosswauld, Adam's brother. The kid, Criss, lovable and interesting as he may be, is an unexpected development. Although, that business of him jumping through a fence has caused some at the Agency to show more than a casual interest, especially since the section of the fence he supposedly jumped through has disappeared. The publicity he has brought to his family is not desirable from the Agency's view."

"You mean your coincidental appearance at the Studlys and the seemingly spontaneous idea to form a defense fund for the Crosswaulds were all planned? How about our friend, the legal guy, Slip Knott; is he a set-up too? I knew there was more to this than met the eye," Pull stated with a tone that suggested his firmness was giving way to anger.

"You played on your friendship with Alice to accomplish a goal for the Agency. Is that the way you treat all your friends?" Pull barked.

"Pull, wake up man, we are at war. Good people are being killed and we must do all we can to head these mad men off. Don't forget the Studlys are law enforcement people and very patriotic, how do you know they weren't in on the plan? I am not saying they were, mind you."

"Yes! We live in a messy world. As I am sure you know, things are often not what they appear to be. Here is the way it is. Jocko and I work, or worked, for the same agency, as does Knott. Jocko was the best of the best at what he did in counter terrorism. He could have been fast-tracked in the highest echelon of the national defense establishment, but he preferred fieldwork; confronting the enemy head-on. Jocko is dead. The enemy thinks they did that deed years ago, but they killed his dad and family instead without knowing it. Operating deep undercover, Jocko penetrated the high command of the terrorists, and spared this nation the grief of several murderous attacks by Islamic extremists. He also brought the mastermind who plotted his death, but killed his family, to swift justice while operating with an assumed identity. The real Jocko was killed recently in a final confrontation with the enemy. I have been authorized to tell you this much, as well as certain details about the actual memorial service if you are interested. The Agency needs your help in keeping a lid on all this attention Criss has brought to the Crosswauld family."

"Of course I am interested, but this seems like a lot of effort to make the bad guys believe they killed Jocko; but not when they thought they did. This doesn't make sense. You know I didn't bargain on all this intrigue when I agreed to help the Crosswaulds," Pull said in a tone he hoped hid the excitement he felt in his gut.

"Am I missing something?" He asked quizzically.

Aggie came back abruptly saying, "You sure are. Get a hold of yourself, Pull, because I am going to blow your mind with this. The reason, at least in part, that the Agency is hustling to keep Jocko's real death a secret has a lot to do with the Crosswauld family's main antagonist. Yes, that would be Hillary Cheatalot. She is not a Muslim, she is a self-proclaimed atheist. The problem is that she is known to have ties to Muslim organizations with extremist views. She has been under surveillance since her anti-war days at WSMU. She seems to have an irrational hatred for everything American. Of the people, for the people, and by the people is abhorrent to her, as are other precepts of the Founding Fathers; including our nation's growth, prosperity, and traditions. She rooted for the Soviets, and when the USSR collapsed, she slipped into the environmentalist movement. Now, she is into radical Islamic stuff. If she discovered the truth about Jocko, the Islamic terrorists would know it quickly. They would shake their organizational tree, so to speak, in a paranoid rage until they uncovered our sources that helped deceive them. Many of our key contacts within the terrorist hierarchy, and no doubt many by-standers, would be in danger of exposure or worse. Those fanatics place no more value on a human life than they do on a goat's life."

Pull, still the skeptic, exclaimed, "That is crazy. Doesn't she know that the terrorists want the Islamic religious law, sharia? They would not even let her walk around with her head uncovered, if they let her walk around at all?"

"You are right, Pull, I think she has been on a mental trip for a long time. She's lost in an unreal, amoral, utopian, dream world, a world that is driven by the worst of mankind's traits: envy, jealousy, deceit, hatred, and a consuming sense of superiority. She is a consummate protestor, and a life-long elitist with a materialistic worldview. In my opinion, she has a mental block between her intellect and her emotions."

Pull interrupted saying, "She surely must know she is flirting with her own self-destruction."

"Yep, that's right. It is sad to say, but there are others who share her ideology. That is what makes the Agency's work necessary, and my job interesting." Aggie replied

"Oh, come on, Aggie, there has to be more to it than that. It just does not make sense that an intelligent woman who serves as a militant, women's liberation advocate is going to be sympathetic with people who believe in having multiple wives and other nonsense, like all those virgins waiting in paradise."

"That is a perplexing challenge you just threw at me, Mr. Itzer. I don't have the answer completely. Everyone is different, of course. But I have put together a profile that seems to pretty well fit women like Cheatalot. They tend to come from upper middle-class backgrounds, are very intelligent, and are socially maladjusted, often with sexual identity issues. Almost without exception, they share a materialistic worldview. You know, a belief that matter is all there is, all there ever was, and all there ever will be. Once a person buys into that notion, it is an easy step to conclude that human beings are just matter like all other creatures. To them, aborting a baby is no worse than what happens to puppies and kittens at the pound. They mask a driving sense of inadequacy with an outward show of superiority. They really don't like people and seem to sense that they were chosen by a natural selection process to be smarter and better than most other people. That strange but all too common view allows them to think of disasters and wars as part of the evolutionary down-select process. Put that thinking together with a strongly held sense of superiority and a desire to fix people and institutions, and you have the making of an elitist mindset. In other words, they think the social order is all fouled up, and everything would be much better if people of their own intellect and point of view were in charge of the affairs of mankind."

"Don't misunderstand me, Pull, I am not saying that all elitists are the same. They seem to come in two predominant mindsets, with a lot of variants. Some of them are tolerant—even benevolent—to those of us who are, in their view, inferior. They toy with us and play us along, much like we would do with the family dog, trainable but not educable, as an old professor of mine once proclaimed. The other elitist mindset seems determined to make the world a better place, in their view, by reducing the number of us inferior specimens and increasing the number of their kind through selective breeding."

"But wait, Aggie, Islamic extremists sure don't seem like good companions for a woman's liberation fanatic."

"Ah! That is where the thinking really gets muddled and downright grandiose. Here is the best theory I have been able to come up with on how all this fits together. There are elitists in every ethnic and religious group. The 'worker-bee' jihadist types and their 'professional protestor class' cohorts are expendable pawns in a game controlled by a small group of uber elitists within the ranks of the Islamic hierarchy, as well as—as strange as it may seem—the ranks of international financial, political, and education circles."

Pull interrupted, "Don't forget the opinion molders in the news media."

Aggie continued while nodding in agreement with Pull's comment. "Once the jihadists and their unwitting associates have done the dirty work and sufficiently disrupted the governments of the world by use of intimidation and sheer terror, the world's leaders will yield to a universal plea for peace and move decisively to bring about order in the world; even if it means adopting a single point of control and authority. That is the end game. The jihadists, et al, can be as passive as a herd of sheep if so ordered by their leaders. For those who don't go along, there is always the sword; a time-honored method of persuasion."

"OK! So you think Hillary Cheatalot is kissing-it-up with these radicals because she believes the elitists among them will calm the jihadists when the time comes; and she will be part of the uber elitists who usher in the New World Order? Do you think she is mad? She must be smart enough to know that, even in the unlikely event that her side prevailed, the odds are definitely against her getting a plumb leadership position in this New World Order. There would be a lot of competition, and some of those competitors have armies and other neat tools of persuasion."

Aggie replied, "You are so right, Itzer, but here is what makes an uber elitist an uber elitist. They think they were deep-picked by a force of nature, or perhaps something on the dark side, to rule humanity. Some call it the 'Great Man Theory.' When driven by a belief that destiny is on their side, logic and intelligence become irrelevant."

"Wow! That is some scary theory you came up with there, Aggie. It sounds like Adolf Hitler, Joe Stalin, and the eugenics crowd would fit right in." Pull uttered with a look of incredulity.

"Ah, come on, Pull, lighten up. Can't you just see her majesty Hillary pontificating from on high?" Aggie said with a huge smile and a laugh to match.

Pull joined in the laughter, which wiped away the focused look of concentration on his face, as he halfway shouted, "Alright, professor, I know I asked for it, but enough already. You're giving me a headache. Let's get back to the situation right here, right now. So, all this secrecy about Jocko explains why the Legal Defense Fund is important to you, or should I say, your Agency?"

"Right on, Pull. Dragging the Crosswauld family into court might inadvertently cause information to come out that would be harmful. As the Agency sees it, the enemy should continue to think they got Jocko when they blew up his family. Keep in mind that the entire Crosswauld family lives with intimate knowledge of Jocko. They know what he did, what he stood for, and how he died, including Criss."

"Go very easy on this, Pull. You are not under oath, but you darn well better act as if you are for both our sakes. And for heaven's sake, keep all that theoretical stuff I just dumped on you, about Cheatalot in particular and elitists in general, to yourself."

Pull quickly said, "Hey, no problem keeping that stuff to myself. You might be on to something here. I'll remember what you have said, but if I can't nail it down with hard facts you won't find it in my commentaries."

"Good! That is what we expected. My comments about elitists and all that was 'off-the-record, background material,' as they say in your profession."

"This patio is a great place for conversation, but we may be overstaying our welcome. Let's meet later and I'll share what I know about Jocko's memorial. I wasn't there. That privilege was for the family and higher-ups. I worked the complex logistics detail and only know what the Agency chose to share, but it must have been a one-of-a-kind event," Aggie added.

CHAPTER 4

Criss's Environment

Pull was contrite after hearing Aggie's explanation as to why she had been so standoffish. This story about Criss Cross had tentacles which reached in many directions like the root of a mighty tree. He had long since learned that things are often not what they appear to be, but this anti-terrorist twist was a shocker. The ramifications could be far-reaching. He was eager to meet with Aggie again to learn more about Jocko, but he was not prepared for the emotional drain it would place on him, a hardened reporter. But for now, he was compelled to continue his quest to unravel the mystery surrounding the Criss Cross phenomenon.

Some of his blog followers had suggested that autistic kids are prone to throw aggressive tantrums and that could explain Criss's behavior. Following up on this suggestion, Pull did another quick review on autism and related neurological disorders which proved to be educational for both he and his followers, but not very useful in understanding Criss.

Pull wanted to interview Criss's doctor but knew medical records would be private. So he persuaded the Crosswaulds to make a special appointment with Criss's doctor, and to allow him to tag along.

Adam introduced Pull saying, "Doctor, I would like you to meet Pull Itzer, you may have seen some of his commentaries about Criss."

The doctor said, "Yes indeed, I have followed your commentaries on the Internet, and I find his exploits to be as interesting as you do. The story about his jumping through a chain link fence really got my attention. As I recall, you said you did not actually see that happen, nor did anyone else."

Pull said, "You are right. No one seems to have seen him actually fly through the fence, all we have is evidence that someone or something did. Can we start with a quick overview of Criss's medical condition?"

"Sure." The doctor looked at Adam for confirmation before continuing, "Criss's condition is not particularly remarkable. There are several shades of autism, and some of my colleagues who like to play with definitions might argue that because Criss has good, if not exceptional, capabilities in certain areas, he does not fit the classic definition. But the treatment is pretty much the same no matter what label is put on it."

"What is the treatment?" Pull asked.

"I never prescribed anything other than a low-dosage medication taken by a countless number of children with attention-deficit hyperactivity," the doctor said.

"No antipsychotic medicines?" Pull asked.

"That's right," the doctor responded.

"Thanks. That is good information for the record," Pull said. "But do you have any idea how he could change from a weak little kid to a super-strong little kid, like turning on a switch?"

The doctor said, "I thought you would ask. It is a logical question, but I honestly don't know. I could speculate, but I won't. The answer, if it can be found, lies beyond the bounds of medical science. As a kid, I learned in catechism that much of what we know intuitively and observe empirically can't be explained scientifically. Given the almost ritualistic nature of his behavior, talking directly to each of the individuals in a commanding manner after each confrontation, suggests that a theologian might be better qualified to tackle the question."

Using every spare minute to do a literature search on the Internet, Pull discovered that there had been studies done that inferred there might be some correlation between autistic behavior and the social environment. He knew the family was rock solid, except for that wild stuff about Jocko Crosswauld. This meant that, just as he had thought from the beginning, he would have to take a hard look at Criss's school environment if he had any chance of answering the big question about what made Criss tick.

Pull determined that Moreville Elementary School was just what one would expect in a peaceful, affluent community. At least that was the way it was when the Crosswaulds moved in. Moreville El, as it was called, had the best of everything according to the local school board, the PTA, and even the town's chamber of commerce. It was well known among insiders in the education and social planning communities because of its celebrated progressive and politically correct approach to all things educational.

Perusal of *Megacity Times* copies in the newspaper morgue file and other public records, coupled with discussions at coffee shops and other gathering places around town, like Bennie's Deli, led Pull to understand that activities at Moreville El were closely intertwined with life in the community. Most of the students' families like Criss's dad either worked in Megacity, the megalopolis down the freeway, or at the local offices of Allypoop Technology, Inc. (APT). APT, the dominant economic power in the community, contributed much to the school system. Some of the students' parents or grandparents were affiliated with APT when it was a mere start-up and became independently wealthy as the company grew. But the children of less affluent, middle-class families like the Crosswalds and Studlys were also well represented at Moreville El. There was nothing unusual about the student body until recently.

Pull learned when something exciting happened, like the new special education program at Moreville Elementary School, the *Megacity Times* was right on it providing a good resource. The pride of the school was the highly publicized program for children like Criss, and the hard-won reputation for being on the cutting edge when it came to socialization.

The Crosswaulds expressed to Pull that the specially trained teachers and state-of-the-art equipment gave them confidence that Moreville El was the right place for Criss, even though he was a reluctant student. They also said that his teacher, Mary Gonzales, assured them that it was typical for children like Criss to resist change.

The program was proving, at least according to the *Megacity Times*, that children with narrow but high order gifts who get individualized attention and careful needs monitoring are better prepared for life as they mature. There was no doubt that Criss had a safe classroom environment, but the playground could be another matter. Pull recalled the words of his old professor in college, "The playground is where some of life's most important lessons are learned." He suspected that a child like Criss would internalize those lessons in a way far different from most kids. As a professional observer of the human condition, he knew the pecking order of dominance naturally places weaker, less aggressive children like Criss on the bottom rung. It would not be easy to fit in with rough and tumble elementary school-age boys, but it is a livable situation. The skills needed to cope are developed and life goes on within the bounds of informal standards of normalcy.

He also knew that all too often one or more of the students are misguided and use coercion to force weaker students into submission. And so it was at Moreville El, even with good supervision and consistent monitoring, educators generally accepted the fact that Criss and others like him had no choice other than to passively accept life as it was. Lunch money and articles of value were sometimes the price the weak paid the strong. Playground bullies could not have known they might have been fertilizing a germ of outrage in Criss's being. From all accounts, Criss was compliant but struggled with a burning desire for justice. His teacher, Mary Gonzales, said, "I could not put my finger on it, but in his own way he seemed to long; not for retribution, but for fairness and justice when subjected to playground abuse."

The Moreville Elementary School PTA was the center for school politics and community-wide social interaction; a fact Pull learned first hand from Eve's account of the Crosswauld family's first exposure to Ms. Hillary Cheatalot, the domineering president of the PTA and noted attorney.

"Only once did I yield to the lingering sense of self-pity for the unfair hand my boy Criss had been dealt," Eve lamented as she told Pull about the conflict with Hillary Cheatalot. "It happened shortly after our family moved to Moreville. Concern for my little boy was a constant companion. It erupted into an uncontrollable mix of rage and hopelessness at a most inconvenient time. Adam was on a business trip. Grandmother Crosswauld was caring for Criss, and Jack was in school. So, I decided to attend a PTA meeting."

"Unbeknownst to me, the major topic of discussion at the meeting was the special education program. This was the first time I had attended a PTA meeting. I was anxious to help. I did not know Hillary Cheatalot, the PTA President, but assumed that all the members shared a common, unselfish interest in the welfare of all the kids in the community."

"Everyone but me seemed to know that Ms. Cheatalot had strong opinions on just about everything and expressed them freely. She seemed to think of her fellow PTA members as being mostly unsophisticated, stay-at-home moms desperately in need of hearing her enlightened worldview. During the discussion, Ms. Cheatalot let it be known that while she supported the special education program because of the progressive nature of it, she held mothers of the unfortunate students who would benefit from the program in great disdain."

Ms Cheatalot stated, "These children are an unnecessary burden on society and that in this time of women's rights, no self-respecting woman should knowingly allow such children to be born."

Eve said, "I was aghast. I had reason to believe that Criss might have a neurological problem but, from my own worldview, abortion was not an option. I never dreamed that a respected leader in my new community with its highly touted reputation for tolerance was so cruel and hypocritical. I burst into tears and ran out of the meeting virtually out of control. In my haste to get to the safety of my home, I hurriedly backed into a car; a brand-new, expensive, foreign-made sedan. No one was hurt. I scarcely noticed it. I was too distraught to leave a note on the car I hit, as I normally would have."

Eve continued, "The crash was not serious, unless the car hit happened to be owned by an attorney of the stature and personality of Ms. Cheatalot. It was technically a hit and run, a fact Ms. Cheatalot made very clear to the police officer who responded to her call; he duly noted her comments on his report which I later saw."

Eve went on to say, "A patrol car arrived at our residence minutes after I burst through the front door leaving our car parked crazily in the driveway. Our household was in turmoil with Adam out of town. My son Jack had just arrived home from high school and became the default crisis manager; a task he handled very well, I might add. He calmly gathered the facts, notified his dad, satisfied the police investigator, and shielded me, his grandmother, and Criss from unnecessary questions or intrusions."

Pull learned from a new friend at Bennie's Deli about a blowup at the PTA meeting saying, "A small crowd had gathered in the Crosswauld's front yard afterwards. After all, one of their kids was strange, and a police car was in front of the house. Some of us were concerned that something serious had happened."

"The police report did note the poise and confidence of young Mr. Crosswauld," Capt. Studly laughingly told Pull in response to his question about the hit and run incident.

Studly went on to say, "That little notation about the good conduct of the Crosswauld kid, Jack, seemed to infuriate Hillary Cheatalot as she eagerly read the report before it was off the preparing officer's desk. While she was in the station, she made it a point to inquire about the background of this family she found so bothersome. She mouthed something about that name, Crosswauld, saying it sounded very familiar."

"I told her that there was a well-known guy with that name who played football," Studly continued. "But she insisted that she had no use for brutal sports like football, so she must have heard the name elsewhere. The entire situation was treated like the overblown, minor incident it was. My guys quickly put it to bed."

Pull, based on what he had learned from Eve and Studly, thought Ms. Cheatalot overreacted. She got her car fixed, as she most certainly knew she would; what more could there be?

After doing a little poking around, Pull found that the issue was not *the* issue. Several attendees at the PTA meeting confided in him that Ms. Cheatalot acted as if she was humiliated by the antics of Eve Crosswauld. Pull reasoned that there was more to it than someone getting upset at a PTA meeting.

He soon learned from casual conversations at Bennie's Deli that his hunch was right. In the wake of Eve's hasty exit, PTA members who knew the Crosswauld family from church gatherings and other neighborhood events dared to challenge the conduct of the PTA President. They even argued that she was out of order, which was like blasphemy since no one had ever challenged her before. One talkative Bennie's customer said, "We should have known what kind of a person she was when she ran for president. She made it clear that she did not need the position but that she would accept it because her prominence as an influential, politically connected lawyer would boost the prestige of the PTA. She said she wanted to 'give back' to the community."

Pull learned that people who knew Cheatalot doubted it was the humiliation that agitated her. It was more likely her fear that when the lightning-fast gossip mill sparked Mrs. James B. More's interest, her chance of full social acceptance would be diminished. Mrs. James B. More was the undisputed society queen of Moreville and a supporter of the sanctity of life movement. Cheatalot was heard to say, "Oh no! Why didn't someone tell me? Those pro-lifers are so narrow-minded that the old Neanderthal will probably hold my comments against me and keep me off the 'A' list."

She must have been burning with anger as she carelessly confided in an associate, who in turn shared it with her hairdresser, a regular at Bennie's Deli. "I truly loath the rich so-and-so and everything she stands for, but acceptance can be a path to the deep-pocket crowd," Cheatalot said. "They all need a lawyer eventually, and with my ACLA contacts in the judiciary, I could do them some good while redistributing as much of their wealth as possible to a more worthy cause. It is just a matter of business; lawyers do what they need to do. It looks like I have some damage control to do, and if I don't get on the 'A' list the Crosswaulds, all of them, will pay."

Pull found all this PTA stuff to be petty, but interesting. He thought it might all tie together as he learned more about life at Moreville Elementary School. It occurred to him that talking to Jack Crosswauld, Criss's brother, might be a good starting point because former teachers remembered him as a kid who obeyed the rules and made friends easily. He received good, but not great, grades and was good enough at all sports to be picked quickly for pick-up games of softball, touch football, and basketball. He seemed to fit seamlessly into the flow of things at Moreville from the first day on campus, just one of the regular guys.

Jack Crosswauld told Pull, "I remember just about everybody was a regular guy with little or no disputes or problems on the playground. Everything seemed normal when I went to Moreville El. I really thought it was a cool place."

Pull inquired, "Did you have trouble with bullies taking advantage of anyone?"

Jack said, "I know there has been trouble with some of the new kids, but I never even thought about it when I went. Oh, guys would push each other and fool around but it was just guys having fun, never had any fights or real trouble."

"Um, it sounds like a different atmosphere than the one Criss and the rest of the current students are facing," Pull thought.

Pull learned from interview after interview that in the few short years since Jack graduated from Moreville El, much had changed. A different set of values came along with the new principal. Some of the parents and older residents of the community openly expressed concern that traditional education had been sacrificed for socialization. Some said that they sensed what used to be right is now considered wrong, and what was considered wrong is now considered tolerable, if not right. What it meant to be a regular guy at Moreville El seemed to have lost its meaning.

Pull looked to Jimmie More to shed some light on campus life these days. He became well acquainted with Jimmie More, who had proven himself to be capable while attending a few meetings with him as interim board members of the Criss Cross Defense Fund. Pull was impressed with Jimmie's candor and ability to function like a mature adult. He was far more sophisticated than most kids his age and from all indications, he was a straight shooter. He was well schooled in the precepts which prevailed when Jack was on campus.

Pull asked Jimmie, "What in the world is going on at Moreville El these days?"

Jimmie responded, "Well, Mr. Itzer, it is kinda hard to say. I don't think anyone really understands the whole picture. Our principle is a bozo who is always mouthing off without really saying much. He brags about being a big-time agent of change, but the biggest change I see is that the unspoken bond of respect for home, family, and authority is no longer self-enforcing. My friends complain when something objectionable happens but look the other way rather than getting involved."

Pull continued, "I have heard a lot of talk about bullies taking over the campus, have you seen bullying? If so, what have you done about it?"

"Ya," Jimmie said. "I guess so, but I can't say I did anything until Criss beat up the biggest bully. He calls himself Billy the Kid, but he is known to everyone else as Billy the Bully. Billy had a run-in with one of my friends about the first day he was on campus. But my friend, who is a pretty big guy himself, told Billy to keep his hands off stuff that did not belong to him, or he would punch him out. That was it, my friends and Billy's friends just ignore each other."

"Jimmie, didn't anyone complain to the principal?" Pull asked.

"Oh, there were a lot of complaints in the beginning, but Mr. Noe Itall called an assembly to tell us we should be tolerant and accept new students without complaining. He sort of blamed us for the trouble because we did not welcome change."

Jimmie's comments hit a nerve with Pull who worried that the low moral standards of the new culture were tempting to young people across the board. He wondered, "What kid would not succumb to the ever-present call for less discipline, less respect for authority, and, to an extent, less respect for the family?" There was no doubt Criss found himself in a vastly different situation than his brother was in as a student at the same school. "Could this have been a factor in Criss's 'explosion of righteousness,' as one observer called his heroic exploits?" Pull mused.

There was a sense of fear on campus that Jack Crosswauld did not have to deal with, but Criss was, from all reports, completely oblivious to any danger. He did not seem to be aware, or care, that those who were not strong enough to stand up to the new crowd would be bullied.

Pull noted on his blog, "It seems an aggressive, almost universal push for socialization has all but eliminated the social bond of the regular guys who unofficially enforced standards of fair play and integrity. The student body is apparently beginning to reflect the attitudes and values of the prevailing culture in Megacity, which borders Moreville like a cancerous growth. Socialization, it seems, brought about an unintended stratification of the student body consisting of regular guys, the gangs, a small isolated group not fitting into either camp, and, of course, the special education kids. Moreville El appears to be transitioning from a source of community pride to a potential powder keg."

Pull had seen this trend elsewhere. Over the years he had reported on several situations in which an unbridled rush to conform to the doctrine of political correctness all but destroyed the very foundation of basic education. Pull sadly reflected on the compromise his alma mater had made on this new altar of conformity and decadence. However, he knew intuitively that, even in the face of a failing education establishment, there were bound to be educators who were in the business for the right reasons. "Moreville El clearly has such educators," he thought as he reflected on Mary Gonzales. He briefly met her the first time he saw Criss and remained impressed with her professionalism as they worked together to help the Crosswauld family defend itself against growing legal threats.

Pull pondered the question, "How do I get this enigmatic woman to help me in my quest to find out what really happened during those confrontations Criss had on campus?" She was, from all indications, the common thread that tied it all together.

CHAPTER 5

Mary's Secret

Pull tried on several occasions to interview Mary Gonzales. Was she really "publicity shy," or was she hiding something as he had sensed when they first met? Each attempt was the same. She was cooperative when it came to superficial facts like names, education, and her official position at Moreville Elementary School. She was also cooperative and informative when it came to discussing neurological disorders. That was it. She guarded information about her personal life like Fort Knox guards the nation's gold. With each direct and even tricky question, she had the ability to give a nice sounding non-answer. It was like interviewing a skilled politician. Her secretiveness irritated Pull.

He would have dropped the whole matter except he felt strongly that Miss Mary, as the kids called her, was a key person in understanding Criss. He had no desire to harm her in any way, but he was determined to continue peeling the skin off the onion, so to speak, just to see what was below the first few layers. Digging out hidden aspects of a person's life can be very difficult, but it can be done, and Pull knew all the tricks.

Mary Gonzales was a highly respected educator with advanced degrees in childhood development. Having done her doctorial dissertation on Pervasive Developmental Disorders (PDD), she was considered one of the foremost authorities on the subject. She was persuaded to leave her teaching position at WSMU to set up and oversee the newly-formed special education program at Moreville El after being assured that she could spend as much time as she felt was necessary interacting with the students. Some decision makers in the education establishment thought it was beneath her when she insisted on performing all the duties of the other special ed teachers, including classroom teaching and especially doing playground duty. She often expressed the notion that the playground is a great social science laboratory which allowed her to interact with and observe her students.

Pull quickly concluded that just as Criss was blessed with a wonderful, caring family, he was also fortunate to have this exceptional teacher in his life. Students, parents, and school administrators alike accepted that Mrs. Mary was firm and fair-minded with particular sensitivity to the needs of the disadvantaged. Pull learned that Criss seemed to feel more secure when Mrs. Mary was in sight, and bullies were less aggressive when she had playground duty. She told Pull, "I thought Criss wanted to communicate his feelings, but he just did not know how. If someone had written what to say for him he could have read it with ease. He has no doubt learned by now though that life is not a TV show with scripts written for every occasion."

Mary went on to say, "Criss is not alone in his private world in which misunderstanding is the norm. There are other broken boys and girls at Moreville El, not just like him, but weak enough to be easy targets for bigger and tougher guys." To illustrate her point, Mary said, "The sight of Betty Honda, a confused girl about Criss's age, being teased to the point of uncontrollable crying, outraged him like I had never observed before. He was really agitated and kept asking, 'Why is she crying? Why is she crying?' Pull, you remember Betty Honda? She is the girl Criss rescued from the pervert the day we met. I never thought of it until now, but maybe there is unspoken communication between them."

"I came to Betty's defense," said Mary. "Trying to show everyone how to deal with a bully, I took the troublemaker—a kid known as Billy the Bully—by the arm and yanked him over in front of Betty Honda. I loudly demanded an apology, not only to Betty but also to all the kids who had gathered around to watch the excitement. I could not let it show, but Billy intimidated me also. He looked and acted like a young man who had brought much sorrow into my life in years gone by. As expected, Billy just laughed and started to cuss and degrade me. At that point—and I am at least a head shorter than Billy—I did an unusual thing for me; I reached up on my tiptoes and grabbed Billy's ear, pulling him close so only he could clearly hear what I had to say. I don't remember exactly what I said, but it worked. Billy reluctantly turned to Betty and repeated word for word exactly what I told him to say. Then, at my insistence, Billy turned to the large crowd of students, teachers, and, by this time, a few administrators and repeated the apology. Billy scurried off smirking. He knew his gang would understand he was just 'jiving the teach.' I got the feeling though that Billy respected me for standing up to him, but, of course, he could never show it."

"Could this have been the tipping point which became a seed of fury and power that later erupted in Criss?" Pull wondered.

Mary went on, "While never claiming to understand him, I felt that somehow we were communicating. As I went about my duties on the playground and in the classroom, it seemed that Criss was always observing me. He had a strange way of looking, but never straight on. On rare occasions, there would be momentary eye contact. It was during those times that I felt a sense of goodness and inner strength radiating from him. This special little boy intrigued me. He was often the subject of conversations with other professionals in my field and also with my own family."

It was well understood that Mary fit nicely into the social fabric of Moreville. Mrs. James B. More liked both she and her husband, a business owner and former professional athlete. They were on the 'A' list for invites to social events held at the More mansion and the country club. The Gonzaleses enjoyed a socially and culturally rewarding life. Life was good, but it had not always been good for Mary. Pull was shocked to learn just how bad Mary had it as a young woman.

Frustrated that Mary refused to talk about her observations of the confrontations Criss had on campus, Pull tried once again to get some insight on what actually went on. It didn't work. She skillfully changed the subject. Her effort to shield all of the students involved, even Billy and his friends, was disturbing. From Pull's perspective, she was a trained observer who had been present when each of Criss's incidents occurred. Her input was essential and the lack of it motivated him to launch a serious background check on this conflicted lady. She had to be hiding something. But what, and why? Even though he feared that he might stumble on something embarrassing, he felt compelled to set his concern for her feelings aside and go after the story.

Her maiden name was a matter of public record. Tapping into his extensive list of contacts compiled during the many years of reporting on life in Megacity, he traced her back to her native village. An informant passed on to Pull that some older villagers remembered Mary, the child who went north, and that she was obsessed with making life easier for handicapped kids. When asked what was meant by being obsessed, no one could explain it; it was just the way she was remembered. A distant relative speculated that it may have been sparked by an incident when she was very young. Jose, a child Mary's age, suffered from a debilitating birth defect that brought him scorn and ridicule. Attending school was out of the question for him. He was ostracized from social functions because he did not fit in. He was different. Jose died at a young age, broken and alone. Mary was remembered because she protested loudly to everyone in the village that Jose died more from the pain of rejection than from his physical condition. She became the center of attention by falling to her knees at Jose's simple funeral and screaming that an injustice had been done. She had prayed loudly that someday she would be able to help kids like Jose. Judging from the career she chose, Pull concluded that helping needy children became her driving passion through many difficult years and tortuous paths.

Word got back to Pull that, in those days, many villagers, even at a young age, knew they would have to leave the village to get an education and pursue their dreams. Mary was remembered as being smart and pretty which caused her mother to admonish her publically to always wear plain, loose fitting clothes and to avoid contact with certain kinds of men. This advice was not easy to follow. As she grew from being a pretty, young girl into a beautiful, young woman, she found herself under the influence of a rugged, ruthless man. He was not much older than Mary, but much more worldly. Her mother pleaded with her and the priest tried to intervene, but the allure of adventure was powerful. She ventured north with her persuasive friend to a "land of opportunity and easy money."

Pull deduced that was the beginning of what must have been the darkest period in her life. According to one of Pull's sources at the Megacity Rescue Mission, that period in her life was a time of abuse and humiliation. She was forced to support the drug habits of her worldly friend by doing things she would never have dreamed of doing in her youthful days of innocence.

Long-time volunteers at the Megacity Rescue Mission remembered Mary or knew something about her because her success was inspirational and proof that they could indeed make a positive difference in a young woman's life. They shared with Pull recollections of how Mary eventually found herself at the door of a clinic for mothers to be. Mary told her rescuers of being despondent and feeling utter despair when her worldly friend pushed her out of his car saying, "Don't worry, I'll be back for you after things are taken care of." She went on to tell people at the Rescue Mission that she was lonely, scared, and desperate as she slowly slouched down the sidewalk to meet her fate. Some older Rescue Mission people remember her saying she was tortured and in anguish at the thought of the horrible thing she was about to do.

Mary told her rescuers, "I hardly noticed the small group of volunteers from the Rescue Mission along the sidewalk until a man in the crowd suddenly reached out to me. I was frightened and disgusted by the thought that even in my condition, another man was grabbing at me. Then, I looked into the face of the would-be assailant and saw something I had not seen since the long journey north began; a kind, gentle face with a warm smile and piercing eyes. I was startled as the man softly said, 'You don't have to do this.' At that moment I felt the presence of others. These kindly women said, almost in unison, 'We have a warm, clean home for you. Come with us.'"

That was the new beginning Mary had hoped and prayed for. An adopted family was found for the child. Mary, after a period of counseling at the home, got a job as a teacher's aide and rediscovered her love of knowledge, all thanks to the man with the kind face and warm smile, Father Mark. It took many hard years of working and attending college part-time before Mary reached the pinnacle of her career.

Visiting the aging priest secretly over the years kept the memories just below the surface. She talked freely about her past on those visits, confident that he would never utter a word about it. Using every trick he knew and every resource at his disposal, Pull eventually knew as much about Mary as Father Mark did. Pull thought, "I have spent all this time and effort piecing Mary's past together, now what am I going to do with it?" The more he learned about her struggles with adversity, the more he admired her. Her courage and motivation would be inspiring to many people. Why couldn't Mary see that? He wanted to help her escape from the bondage of guilt. He did not know how until his investigation led to Father Mark. Pull shared what he had learned about Mary with Father Mark and asked if it would be advisable for the three of them to meet.

Pull, Mary, and Father Mark gathered in a small, secluded study. Pull revealed to Mary what he knew about her past and assured her that Father Mark was not the source of his information. With Father Mark's concurrence, he pleaded with her to come to the understanding that her story could be a liberating experience for herself and an inspiration for other young women caught up in the same sorry circumstances she had faced.

Father Mark said, "Mary, you know the truth will set you free. In your own time and in your own way, you must tell your story. You owe it to the ones you love, you owe it to those who could benefit from hearing it, and most importantly, you owe it to yourself."

Mary reached for the tissue box that had thoughtfully been placed on the table in front of her. Tears of relief flowed freely. Wiping her face between sobs, she thanked Father Mark and Pull for showing her the error of her thinking in trying to block out the past.

Mary later told Pull, "I thought I had successfully suppressed the lingering emotional scars of those difficult years, but I never forgot the journey. I felt that, as brutal as it had been, it made me a more compassionate and caring wife, mother, and educator. It all happened so long ago; I thought the memories had been safely locked away in my mind, but I knew better. It was like living a lie; even my husband, whom I love dearly, does not know about that hard journey north and the nights on the streets."

She went on to tell Pull, "I thought my secret was safe and that it would never be revealed, but I was fearful that my success and the press attention brought about by Criss would be my undoing. A snooping reporter like you could start asking embarrassing questions. My whole professional life reflects a wholehearted belief that the truth is always the best policy. But my fear and latent guilty feelings were so great that I mistakenly believed that my career and family life would be ruined if the truth about my past were known."

CHAPTER 6

Billy the Bully

Pull had heard a lot about this kid. He was a notorious troublemaker like so many he had encountered in the past. At first, he thought he would not even bother with this punk. Who needs it? Then he remembered the police reports Captain Studly had shared with him on each of the incidents involving Criss. Billy Benez was the one who triggered Criss's first winning confrontation against seemingly insurmountable odds. "Who knows," he thought, "I might find an insight about Criss by turning over a few stones to see what this kid is all about."

Those who knew Billy's background willingly shared with Pull about his troubled life. He did not become a student at Moreville El in the usual way. He had become part of the student body because of a socialization experiment which was eagerly endorsed by a vociferous collection of educrates, political activists, and timid politicians.

Billy did not live in Moreville and did not want to be at Moreville El. He really did not want to be in any school. He preferred the streets of his neighborhood. But it did not matter what he wanted, or what the parents in his neighborhood wanted. The unwritten rules of political correctness had to be followed.

Some students at Billy's old school were in need of special education facilities. However, the Megacity School Board readily admitted they were not only disinclined, but incapable of providing such facilities to them. Social engineers, a ubiquitous collection of people educated far beyond their intelligence, observed that Moreville was not the ideal diverse community; therefore, Moreville El students were being deprived of the wonderful opportunity to "celebrate diversity." A few meetings here and there, numerous editorials in the *Megacity Times* extolling the virtues of school busing to achieve socialization, and one day it happened. Billy found himself, along with many other kids from his old school in Megacity, on a bus headed for Moreville. A few of those from Billy's old school did need the special education offered at Moreville El, but most did not. In the eyes of social planners, it was a win-win situation. Megacity would be helped with its need for a good special education program, and Moreville would at last solve its perceived need to be more like the big city down the freeway. The special education angle was a convenient ploy to persuade anti-busing people in both communities to buy into the plan.

According to Pull's ever growing group of fans, Moreville leaders like Ms. Cheatalot could publicly claim school busing was a matter of reaching out to help the disadvantaged. At social gatherings, which were always covered by the *Megacity Times*, they could brag about the good deed they had done for the "poor folks." Plenty of glowing quotes on the society page could be expected. An added plus for certain members of the Moreville leadership crowd was that pulling off this politically desirable feat without having any of "those people" actually live in Moreville, gave them an occasion for mutual backslapping behind closed doors.

Pull had a good sense of what this kid, Billy the Bully, was all about, but he needed to talk to him directly. He went to the principal, Noe Itall, for advice about talking to Billy, and he received a flat rejection. "No interviews allowed, not with Billy or any other student assaulted by Criss Crosswauld."

"OK, Mr. Noe Itall, but may I ask why? And besides, it isn't clear to me who assaulted whom?" Pull responded.

"It is very simple," was the reply. "You will have to talk to his lawyer," as he handed Pull a business card bearing the names; Sleazer, Bagman, Ahmad, and Cheatalot."

Pull had an urge to lean on this guy, Mr. Noe Itall, but thinking better of it, he excused himself and began to conjure up a way to talk to Billy without an attorney's permission. As he thought about his options, he remembered that Mary Gonzales had some sort of an off-campus social gathering for a few students at Moreville El. Since his already good rapport with Mary was even better after their meeting with Father Mark, he decided to approach Mary about sitting in on one of her socials with the kids.

"Mary, I don't ordinarily invite myself to other people's parties, but I sure would like to sit in the next time you have Billy included in an off-campus meeting," Pull said in a voice that made it hard for Mary to refuse.

Mary said in mock surprise, "You really are a snoopy reporter. I won't ask how you found out about my practice of taking three or four kids to the local fast-food place once a week. It is my way of adding an extra dimension to the on-going evaluation of how my special education students mix with other kids in a non-threatening setting. Sometimes I even invite a few kids over for a swim party on weekends. I have included Billy from time to time and I think it might be about time to invite him again; he always seems eager to join in. I think you will find that he is an interesting kid."

Pull said, "Thanks, Mary. That will be Helen's Heavenly Hamburgers this Thursday?"

To which Mary exclaimed with the kind of charm that made her popular, "You sneaky devil! Do you know everything about me? See you Thursday."

Pull learned from a friendly administrator in the school district that the Benez kid was more than the Moreville El staff was prepared to handle. "He was older, bigger, and much more street-wise than any other student at the school," the staffer said. "All of us knew that Billy's family was anything but normal by Moreville standards, but not so by the standards accepted in his own neighborhood. Billy, like many of his friends, did not have a father in the home. Some of us thought he did not even know who his father was. Public assistance had been cited in the transfer records as the family's source of income." Pull's new friend went on to say, "Administrators in the Megacity School District were not sure about his real name. The name and address on his records changed frequently. He was accused of making up the name 'Billy' because he admired Billy the Kid, you know the bad guy in the Old West. No one seemed to know his real age or education background either. Some thought he should have been in high school because of his size and appearance." Shaking his head, the administrator went on, "As crazy as it was, he was accepted without a challenge because it might have agitated Ms. Cheatalot, who made a handsome income as a civil rights litigator, if we did not. Around here no one bucked her, Billy's rejection could have been considered discrimination, and she could have had us in court demanding huge compensation for his mental anguish, or whatever she dreamed up."

Even though Billy had a reputation as a gang leader, the decision was made to accept his transfer by Moreville El's principal who stated, "Billy will soon learn the ways of civil behavior and adjust to the norm at Moreville El."

It soon became apparent from conversations on and off the Moreville El campus that even some of the most liberal of the educrates regretted Mr. Noe Itall's decision. Graffiti began to appear on the campus, and all the students—as well as most of the teachers and staff—knew that Billy's gang members hung out at the door to the restrooms demanding money for entrance. They pounced on students who appeared weaker like a pack of wolves pouncing on a stranded sheep. Kids in the special education program were the most vulnerable.

It did not take long for the few disciplinarians at Moreville El to declare Billy incorrigible. It seemed jail time was a certainty in Billy's future.

Mary knew all the background stuff in addition to her own observations about Billy, and was apprehensive about inviting him to social meetings. She did so because he was the leader of the troublemakers, and she wanted to observe how he acted when not under pressure from his peers to be a tough guy.

Pull arrived early at Helen's place and arranged to have the bill for Mary's group discreetly given to him. Pull said, as if he were surprised, "Well hello Mrs. Gonzales, it's nice to see you. And who are these folks?"

Mary took the cue and introduced Pull as a reporter. Billy seemed impressed to be in the company of someone so important, a point that didn't go unnoticed by Pull. He asked if he could join them while simultaneously slipping into a seat next to Billy.

Billy asked, "Are you a real reporter?"

Pulled answered, "Yes, I am. I have written stories about many famous people."

"That must be a neat job. Are you going to write a story about school?" Billy asked.

Pull replied, "Billy, I have been writing and talking about the things that have been going on at your school for a while now. Would you like to tell me about Moreville El?"

"Ya man, I would be a big man in the hood if you talked about me and the guys saw the story. But I am not supposed to talk to anyone."

"Oh man, that's too bad! How come you can't talk about school?" Pulled said, as if he were really disappointed.

Billy said, "I don't know why I can't talk about school, but a lawyer told me and my mom that we could get a lot of money if I just keep my mouth shut. I think she said it about three times, and told my mom to sign some papers so she could represent me. I remember she said that we would be really happy because she always wins, and that could mean we would get big bucks; but, I had to do exactly as she said. The other guys from the hood who go to Moreville El were told the same thing."

"Well, I don't want you to get in trouble with your lawyer. Who is your lawyer anyway?" Pull asked.

"Ah, I don't know, I think it is Hillary something. I see her at school once in a while. Usually, when I am in the vice principal's office getting yelled at, she is in the principal's office. If she sees me she always tells me to keep quiet about anything that happens at school, or anything that has to do with Criss Cross."

CHAPTER 7

The Mysterious Uncle Jocko

Pull, trying to sort out the sequence of events that led up to the beginning of Criss's superhero adventures, talked extensively with Adam. The conversations were guarded. Pull didn't want to be abrupt, as reporters often are. After all, according to Aggie, Adam and his entire family had every right to be sensitive with lingering feelings of remorse. Pull approached the subject gingerly saying, "Hey, Adam, do you mind if I ask you a few questions about your brother Jocko, strictly off the record? I know it is a very delicate situation. I have been given a light briefing by the Agency, and I think I know about his death. It seems like he was such a remarkable person, and I would like to know about the man; for my own edification, not for publication, of course."

Adam looked shocked; giving Pull a sense that maybe broaching the subject at this time was inappropriate. Then Adam, after a reflective pause, replied in a calm, subdued manner, "So, you want to know about the mysterious Jocko, do you? OK! I can talk about Jocko. But first you need to know that he was not mysterious, but his job sure as heck was. Talking about him might even be therapy of a sort."

"To start with, he was a big guy; probably a couple of inches taller than you, but much better looking of course." That brought a good-natured laugh from both men. Adam went on to say, "Jocko was a senior in high school when I was a freshman. I idolized him. He was exceptional in academics, sports, and everything else he did. One of my fondest memories is of the family—dad, mom, Jocko, and me—sitting at the kitchen table talking about Jocko's options after high school."

"It seemed like every college in the country wanted him. There were so many coaches trying to recruit him that it became disruptive. A decision had to be made. The decision Jocko made will tell you all you need to know about his character. Recruiters were saying that no matter which college he chose, a brilliant football or baseball career and an excellent education lay ahead. If professional sports were not appealing after graduation, they argued that his education would equip him for other fields of endeavor. Jocko asked Dad, 'What do you think I should do?' Before Dad could respond Mom said, 'Wait a moment. Let's pray about this thing.' We prayed about everything in our house. Dad then asked Jocko, 'Son, what do you think you want to be doing in four or eight years? What do you think would be the most satisfying?' To which my brother said, 'Well, I am not really sure, but I actually felt better about my accomplishments after last summer's missionary trip to Asia than I did about getting the most valuable player award after the state championship football game.' 'Son, don't you think that tells you something important?' Dad asked. My brother said, 'Yes, I think it does. I would like to do some kind of work that would be a service to mankind.' Mom seemed to beam as Dad said, 'OK, let's narrow the choices down. Which of these institutions is the most likely to give you a chance to play highly competitive sports while preparing you for a career of service?' As Jocko pondered the question, Dad added, 'You know you could do a lot worse than accepting the Academy appointment.' Dad continued with a big smile that bordered on a laugh, 'You know I am not saying that because I am a Marine vet who bleeds red, white, and blue.' We all burst into a spontaneous chuckle as my brother said, 'I read you, Dad, loud and clear.'"

"That was it. You mentioned earlier that you followed his football accomplishments, the All-American award and so forth. Pro-football scouts were trying to sign him to play after his military obligation was fulfilled. He truly loved the game and gave some thought to playing pro ball, but some place along the way he came to realize that it was just a game played to entertain people. Being an entertainer was OK for some folks, but it just wasn't his calling."

Pull interjected, "So your brother was a team player in the finest sense of the expression; equally comfortable in the background, or out in front?"

"Yep! That about nails it, Pull. He certainly was not driven by ego, far from it."

Pull continued, "As you know, Adam, I have been rattling around trying to piece events together hoping that I could shed a little light on what drives Criss."

"Boy, that would be an accomplishment. A lot of people are wondering what is going on with Criss. Have you heard the rumors that he takes a 'magic' pill developed by Allypoop Technology?" Adam asked.

"Ya! I think I have heard them all. People sure have active imaginations," Pull responded. "So, if you don't mind, Adam, tell me what life was like around your house before you learned about Jocko's death?"

"Well, why don't I start with the commotion caused by Hillary Cheatalot's confrontation with Eve at the PTA meeting and the subsequent visit from the Moreville police? Jack, my teenage son, filled me in on the telephone in such detail that I felt assured a crisis had been avoided. Nevertheless, I desperately wanted to get back home from a business trip, so I cut the trip short and headed home ASAP."

"When I arrived, I found that Jack had indeed managed the situation well. All was calm at the Crosswauld household. My mom lived with Jocko in his condo in Megacity, but was staying with Eve and the boys in Moreville while I was gone. She enjoys the grandkids and frequently visits. It gives her a much desired opportunity to talk to the boys."

"I think Mom hardly noticed my arrival. She was engaged in what had become a preoccupation in recent years, deep conversations with the family about Jocko. My mom knew a lot about Jocko's life; often saying that her knowledge about his exploits, vast as it was, could be compared to a bucket of water next to an Olympic-sized swimming pool. We were all haunted to some extent by the knowledge that, through no fault of his own, Jocko's work brought about the brutal murder of my dad and Jocko's wife and children. The memory of that dreadful event hung heavily over the entire family, especially my mom. It gave rise to an uncharacteristic sense of urgency in her storytelling. She would, on rare occasions, talk of her fear that sooner or later they would kill Jocko and perhaps even do further harm to the rest of his family."

Adam went on to say, "My mom reasoned that if she did not pass on the knowledge she had to the family, there might not be anyone aware of Jocko's remarkable stories of heroics and sacrifice. She was concerned that even though Jocko painstakingly recorded his activities in a coded journal, the people he worked for would never let the truth out. They insisted that his every move was classified as top secret and would probably remain so for fifty years." Adam added, "Mom's desire to talk about Jocko was enhanced by the certain knowledge that she was getting older, and my brother's life was in constant danger. She felt compelled to share as much as she could without breaching the security clearance she had been given when she moved into his condo in downtown Megacity."

"Mom was persuaded to live with Jocko for security reasons. Jocko's superiors felt that it would be safer for her and easier for them to conceal the fact that Jocko was still alive. The Agency wanted her shielded from the public, especially reporters and others who might want to know what happened to her football-playing son. There was always a chance that she might let something slip out."

"It was more of a monologue than a conversation when I came into our family room that evening. Mom was regaling the boys with stories about Jocko's accomplishments and high adventures. Like I said, I loved and greatly admired my big brother, but I got a little tired of hearing about his athletic and academic accomplishments. I had to admit to myself that I felt a slight tinge of jealousy growing up in the shadow of Jocko, as I listened to Mom in her engaging manner."

"Hearing about Jocko's clandestine life as a top secret agent in charge of anti-terrorism was as intriguing to me as it was to the boys. There was much Mom did not know, and there was much she did know but could not reveal. She shared that she was shocked to find out just how strange Jocko's lifestyle was when she moved into his bunker-like condo on the top floor of the tallest building in Megacity. She said he was gone a lot of the time, and when he was home there seemed to be weird things going on. He wore all kinds of disguises as he came and went. At first she was not sure who was coming through the front door. The Agency solved that problem quickly with electronic identification hardware."

Pull later learned that the top floor had been chosen by Jocko's superiors because it had a concealed heliport and chopper at the ready. This extraordinary security was necessary to conceal one of its biggest secrets; Jocko was alive.

Pull checked out the news stories covering Jocko's supposed death. The media accurately reported that four people had been killed in a car bombing at the suburban Washington, D.C. home of Mr. Jack Crosswauld, a government employee. The driver of the car was identified as Jack Crosswauld; other victims were his wife and two children. Family members were just collateral damage to the terrorists. What the media did not know was that Jack had the same name as his father. Jack's father was driving the car. First responders had only his charred wallet to ID the remains. Jocko's superiors allowed the story to stand uncorrected, leading the terrorists to believe they had been successful.

Adam went on to say, "I never understood why the Agency insisted that the family keep quiet about the incident. You can't imagine how hard that was. I reasoned that the terrorists' blunder turned out to be beneficial in a strange way, understood only by Jocko and his superiors."

"Jocko was now forced to live a much more complicated life as an agent without a real name. This was a burden he readily agreed to in the hope that being incognito would allow him to adopt more creative plans to trap the perpetrators of this and other heinous, inhuman acts of terrorism."

Adam continued, "I had another reason to listen to my mom tell the family of Jocko's hair-raising adventures and Jocko's near-superhuman escapes from danger. I knew a special bond between Criss and Jocko had been formed very early in Criss's disturbed life. The bond seemed to strengthen since the loss of Jocko's own two children. I could sense it and observe it, but like so much in Criss's behavior, it was not comprehensible."

"Jocko had little time for family get-togethers. Since the death of his family, he devoted himself more than ever to fighting Islamic terrorism. He let us know that his personal goal was to look the evil men, who ordered the unsuccessful attempt on his life, in the eyes before extracting revenge from each of them. It was a consuming passion of his."

"He feared for the safety of the remaining family so much that he usually met us at mountain retreats. Even then, he was unrecognizable to the family until he spoke. On the rare occasions when Jocko visited Moreville, he dressed up like a repairman or a gardener. Strangely, Criss was always the first one to see through the disguise. It was great fun to see Criss break the news to the rest of us as he invariably ran to Jocko with abandon."

"Only once did our family ever visit Mom and Jocko at Jocko's condo. Mom told us that they both wanted to show us, especially the kids, the strange and interesting place. My son Jack immediately dubbed it the 'cave in the sky.' No matter where it was held, mystery and intrigue surrounded a visit with Jocko. It was high adventure for the whole family."

Adam reflected, "When Jocko's name came up in family conversations, Criss's demeanor changed dramatically. He came out of his self-imposed isolation, seeming to internalize in some strange way every word uttered. At times, he repeated stories told about Jocko in amazing detail. It was as if I was listening to a tape recording with precise voice inflections and tone."

"Mom's great gift for storytelling made her an excellent conduit from Jocko to the rest of our small family. It gave me pleasure and hope to see Criss so totally focused and capable of asking his grandma penetrating questions. No other activity stimulated Criss like this. The whole Crosswauld family hoped and prayed that some force was at work within Criss which would enable him to eventually outgrow his developmental disorder."

CHAPTER 8

Last Good-bye to Uncle Jocko

True to her word given at the More mansion following Criss's Legal Defense Fund board meeting, Aggie arranged to meet with Pull to share the details about Jocko's demise and memorial service. They met in Pull's small, extended-stay hotel suite, which he had converted into a makeshift newsroom. The little apartment was like a man cave with a large Moreville map tacked to a wall. The map attracted Aggie's attention immediately. Pull, or someone, had carefully highlighted certain streets with peculiar code-like comments at various locations. Aggie couldn't help herself. She blurted out, "Pull, you either have a strange way of decorating or something is going on here. What's with this map?"

Pull broke into a laugh as he exclaimed, "Don't be so suspicious, Aggie. That map helps me remember the interesting places I see, and the people I meet while jogging."

"Hey, Pull, I didn't know you were a jogger. It never showed up in your file." The idea that the Agency had a file on him kind of ticked Pull off, but he thought better of voicing his discontent to Aggie. Instead, he fired back saying, "Since you know all about me, why don't you tell me about you?"

Feeling a little threatened she said, "I guess that's fair, but I really don't have much to say. I joined the Agency as an intern after college. My life has been filled with tedious, demanding challenges mixed in with periods of exhilaration and boredom. I soon learned that normal family life was not an option. I guess I kind of married the Agency."

Pull, sensing he may have hit a nerve, quickly got the conversation back on neutral ground by saying, "Here's the deal about my jogging which is kind of a new routine for me. After my wife passed away, I had to get active so I tried jogging and found it to be something I really enjoyed, especially in this great weather. Those marked streets are my jogging paths. Notice they all start and end at the place with the circled number one. That is Bennie's Deli just down the street from here. I start and end my morning jogs at Bennie's. Jogging gives me a good sense of the pulse of the community. I have developed a nodding acquaintance with several commuters as they head off to work. I am on a first name basis with many of the shop owners and workers on Main Street. It seems that several local folks follow my commentaries and make it a point to drop by Bennie's Deli in the mornings for bagels, coffee, and conversation. It is a traditional social gathering place around here. Bennie, the owner, jokingly says that he doesn't know or care what I do, but if business keeps picking up, he will think about giving me a commission. I have learned a lot of stuff about this fair town and the people who make it their home. Bennie's is a great place to gather background information and to calibrate some of the local personalities."

It was the first time Pull and Aggie had been alone, *really* alone. Aggie assured him that she wasn't wearing a wire, and Pull assured Aggie that he did not care. Laughing, she quickly added, "It would not matter anyway. Anyone who might be listening knows what I know already, and they probably wouldn't believe what you might say; so there."

"OK kiddo, enough of this hilarity. Let's get down to business."

"You are right, Pull. Well, here is everything I know—or everything I am free to tell you—about Jocko's last good-bye, as they reverently refer to it at the Agency."

Aggie cautioned Pull, "It is from the personal journal that Adam was instructed to keep, plus copious notes kept by Agency observers, that allow me to fill you in on the intimate details of those sorrowful days. Pull, you do have a security clearance, but you would never have access to this if it were not for your unexpected involvement with the family. You are never to relate any of this to anyone. I hope you know that is not exactly a warning, but it is much more than a plea."

Aggie told how the family, especially Grandma Crosswauld, lived in constant fear that one day Jocko would be taken out by the enemy. That dreaded message came in the form of a man dressed as a refrigerator repairman at the Crosswauld's residence in Moreville. The messenger had thoughtfully arranged to have all of Jocko's remaining family present when he sorrowfully and respectfully told of Jocko's last act of extreme heroism. The story had an overwhelming finality, unlike those grandma may have told. The messenger noted that the family expressed a full range of emotions; Mrs. Crosswauld lapsed into a period of silence followed by sobs as she moaned, "I have now lost my son as well as my daughter-in-law, two grandchildren, and my husband in this war. Will the sorrows ever end?" He noted, "I stayed late into the evening trying to console them, a task I had been trained to do, but I fear my effort was grossly inadequate. The emotions were overwhelming."

The messenger had complete details of how the final memorial service would be held, which, like everything else in Jocko's life, was complicated. He outlined the plans and assured the family that everything was subject to the family's approval. He pointed out that the bad guys did not know who they had killed, and

Jocko's superiors wanted to keep it that way. The memorial service was to be held on the roof of Jocko's condo. It would be a full military funeral, less the twenty-one gun salute. The messenger explained that Jocko's reputation was such that dignitaries from the highest echelons of various security agencies, including some from foreign countries, would be there to express their condolences and to say a few appropriate words. He made a point to tell the Crosswauld family that the President would send a high-level emissary to bestow the highest medal the country had on Jocko posthumously. Notes indicate that the family must have been in shock because they seemed less impressed with that great honor than would ordinarily be expected. The messenger stressed that the entire event would be kept secret as a matter of national security, but that family wishes would take precedence. He also said that the family need not worry about details of the memorial and that necessary changes to Jocko's condo and logistical issues were already being worked out. "That is where I came in," Aggie said. "Planning and logistics are part of my job description."

Aggie shared with Pull, "The Crosswauld family again was swept up in events not of their own choosing. Grandma let it be known that she would have preferred a much simpler, private, memorial service, as would have Jocko. She was reluctant to go along with the Agency's plan. It was her right and she knew it. It was Adam who reminded his mom that with Jocko, in death as it was in life, it was always a matter of duty, honor, and country. He gently persuaded his mom that it was the right thing to do by telling her the family should allow a memorial that would be the most honoring to Jocko's life, and that the Agency could be trusted to do it with dignity. All it took to placate her was assurance that, even though it would be conducted by a military chaplain, it would be a traditional Christian service."

"As the day for Jocko's memorial approached, the entire Crosswauld family moved into Jocko's spacious 'cave in the sky,' an expression picked up by Agency staffers from Jocko who got it from his nephew Jack. The carefully planned move eased logistics problems and gave the family time to be together in Jocko's world preparatory to the service. The family arrived the same way it had been done the other time they visited Jocko's place. They parked the family car in a designated parking stall in the adjacent building, and proceeded to Jocko's building through an underground tunnel. The tunnel led to an express elevator that speedily took them to a corridor two floors below Jocko's floor. Once in the corridor, they went into an ordinary looking office that had another inconspicuous elevator which took them up to Jocko's floor. From there, it was a short walk down another corridor to a large door with fancy, engraved letters. The lettering indicated that it was a business of some kind, but behind the large door was Jocko's 'cave in the sky.' Security people using yet another elevator discreetly handled the family's luggage."

Pull asked, "How did these guys at the Agency maintain the tight security they seemed to be fixated on with all this activity?"

"Good question. I didn't have a need to know, that's just the way it works. I do know that an Agency security specialist had been directed to brief Adam, to the extent necessary. He was also instructed to inform him that, as a matter of security, he would be requested to keep a journal on all activity in the condo, no matter how trivial it might seem. Yes, even the activity of his children would have to be recorded. Records indicate Adam protested that the request was unreasonable but agreed to comply. The security specialist informed Adam that there were cameras, but for the family's privacy, cameras were only activated at points of entry. The security guy indicates in the record that he was uncomfortable laying this burden on Mr. Crosswauld and tried to explain that in a highly secured facility, rules are inflexible."

Aggie went on to say, "This is very personal, but because of your intense interest in Criss, I will share with you what Adam noted in his journal. 'Once inside the condo, the family gathered in front of a huge display case that contained Mom's treasures; trophies, awards, pictures of both of us boys, and her grandkids in football, baseball, and other sport's uniforms. There was also a featured place for Jocko's numerous war medals and citations. All of us focused on this part of the display case, especially Criss. He stood silently as I read the citations which accompanied each of the medals. They told story after story of uncommon valor. Mom quickly reminded us that it was not like Jocko to put such items on display. It was all her doing, and she had never been more proud of her son than she was at this time.'"

Aggie continued, "Here is a notation from Adam's journal you will find particularly interesting. 'As the family settled in for the night, I noticed that Criss was missing from bed. I instinctively knew I would find him at the display case. I was not prepared for the heartbreaking sight. There was my broken little boy, who had previously shown very little emotion about anything, sobbing uncontrollably. He knew his Uncle Jocko was gone, and that a bad guy had made it happen. He seemed to want to touch the medals. I impulsively opened the case and took one of the medals out for Criss to hold. He ran to his bed clutching the medal with both hands, leaving me to ponder if I had done the right thing. After discussing what I had seen and done with Mom, she quickly agreed that the medal should stay with Criss.'"

Aggie related to Pull that all reports indicated that the day of the memorial service was tense. "Everything went off like the precise military operation it was. There were many men with stars and bars and numerous campaign ribbons on their uniforms. One of the men, with a chest full of campaign ribbons on his immaculate uniform, was the messenger who pretended to be the refrigerator repairman. He made a point to tell each member of the family that, even though this service never officially happened, he understood it would be almost impossible to keep it a secret if someone was determined to find out about it. They were not expected to lie, but they were strongly urged not to volunteer anything to anyone; especially someone claiming to be an investigator or reporter. Not even personal friends casually inquiring about the once famous athlete Jocko Crosswauld should be told."

Aggie was instructed to read this statement provided by the Agency for Pull's ears only. She did so in a subdued, almost reverent tone:

> *NOTE: This event is classified SECRET and is to be treated accordingly until officially declassified. Many of Agent Crosswauld's colleagues told about events in his extraordinary career, even at the risk of revealing information that had not been officially declassified. All in attendance were enlightened. His mother, Mrs. Crosswauld, seemed surprised and shocked to learn how important his work had been to the security of the United States. Mrs. Crosswauld displayed symptoms of severe distress. Her grief was no doubt magnified by memories of her husband, daughter-in-law, and two grandchildren who were murdered by the same Islamic terrorists who killed her son, Agent Crosswauld. Even at this time of anguish, which could only be expressed with deep, sorrowful sobs, she remained dignified as did her only other child, Adam Crosswauld and his family, comprised of his spouse, Evelyn, and two children, Jack and Criss. Your Point of Contact (POC) is Agent Agatha Etsirhc. Said agent is authorized to reveal information the Agency deems appropriate and no more. Do not inquire further.*

After a poignant pause, Aggie shared Adam's cryptic, barely legible notes. "The utter solemnness of the ceremony brought each one of our remaining family to a point of tearful reflection. In our own way, we all knew that my brother Jocko was a good and decent man who gave his life in the line of duty, and in doing so, saved countless others. Our family had made tremendous sacrifices in the war on terrorism, and we were consoled to hear each speaker acknowledge the unbearable burden we had borne. Each of us felt a sense of pride, but the price was higher than one family should have to pay. This ceremony and the eloquent comments brought things into perspective. All of us were visibly shaken, especially Criss. I had never seen him so focused before."

Combining Agency notes with notes from Adam's journal, Aggie continued cautiously because she feared her respect for Jocko would cause her emotions to allow more information to slip out than Pull needed to know. "It was a fitting and memorable service cloaked with symbolism, especially the flag-draped coffin with the Medal of Honor and Jocko's personal, pocket New Testament carefully placed on top. All in attendance were emotionally impacted, some to the point of being drained. At the conclusion of the service, attendees quietly milled about; many approached the coffin to either salute or just stand at attention with their heads bowed. Before long they had all risen, except Criss who was sitting like a frozen figure grasping a medal." Adam noted, 'Criss remained focused on the coffin in spite of Eve's gentle urging to stand up and join the rest of us in a makeshift reception line. When Criss did respond to Eve, he stood straighter than ever before, as if he had grown a few inches. He was not the same little boy who cried profusely at Mom's display case. He remained locked-in on the flag-draped coffin without saying a word.'"

Aggie struggled to contain the urge to cry as she told Pull, "Agency notes report that a high ranking officer said that the boy looked like a top-notch quarterback in a must-win game. He had his game-face on."

After a reflective pause Pull haltingly said, "Jocko's last good-bye was truly overwhelming to those who knew him, especially for the family. I had no idea what they went through. The pain must still be intense and to think they have kept it all inside during my many discussions with them, what a family! Thanks for briefing me, Aggie. It does explain the unusual attraction Criss has for the medal he keeps with him. Do you mind if I ask a question?"

"No, just don't poke at anything that might reveal specific details about who attended, where, when, stuff like that."

"I took the admonition seriously. As you folks say, I don't have a need to know. I would like to get your opinion on how and why Criss turns his body into a human torpedo, but only to right a wrong. I know you were a psychology major, and your profession must have exposed you to a lot of weird things."

"Well, Pull, I did earn a masters degree in clinical psychology and you are right I have seen and read about some very strange things, some even suggesting supernatural intervention, but I have never heard of a physical object like a medal acting as a trigger mechanism enabling the bearer to exhibit great feats of strength. I do, however, believe the capabilities of the human mind and the spiritual dimensions we human beings possess are virtually limitless. Anything is possible, especially for those who have a simple abiding faith."

CHAPTER 9

The Transformation and Day of Reckoning

Pull realized that he knew far more about Criss—thanks to the story Aggie had shared about Criss's uncle Jocko—than did anyone else outside of the immediate family, and the Agency, of course. He could pursue his quest to learn what made Criss tick with privileged insight, which brought with it a sense of anxiety that he himself might inadvertently reveal information that could be passed on by terrorist sympathizers. This new knowledge about the Crosswauld family tragedy, especially about Criss's reaction to the loss of his uncle Jocko, motivated him to push even more vigorously to tie the whole story together. Mary Gonzales was the key to obtaining a more accurate account of what really happened on that eventful day when Criss encountered Billy the Bully. It was not easy. She was still fearful about her past being exposed.

Finally, Pull put aside his sympathy for Mary's feelings and sternly said, "Come on Mary, this is serious. I just might have a clue as to where or how Criss gets his power. Don't forget Father Mark's admonition about the truth setting you free. If your past is made known because of your involvement with Criss, it will just help you fulfill the commitment you made. It will make it easier to reveal your experiences to your family and friends, if not to the public. Be strong, Mary. You could add a much-needed insight to the puzzle."

"All right, Mr. Ace Reporter, you win." Mary responded with a good-natured smile and shoulder shrug. "I will give you the interview you have been bugging me about, but I want you

81

to know that I am not so much impressed with your persistence as I am with the plight of the Crosswauld family. If my talking about Criss's playground encounters with Billy and the others will in anyway help the Crosswaulds, I'll do it gladly. After all, I am an interim member of the Board of Directors of the Criss Cross Defense Fund, thanks to your maneuvering. I know you pushed the Mores to appoint me, you sly devil. Just kick back and take a listen."

"I am all ears," Pull responded with a satisfied grin spreading across his face.

Matching Pull's smile with one of her own, Mary began, "Here is what I have deduced along with what I witnessed. The Crosswauld family took Criss with them after being called away. Presumably, it was to attend a family funeral. There was little time for the family to adjust to the loss of their loved one before having to serve the demands of work, school, and life in general. The first day Criss came back, he seemed about the same. I did not notice anything unusual except he did have what appeared to be a war medal in his possession that I had never seen before."

"Did you see the medal, Mary?"

"Yes. I did ask him where he got it, but I didn't understand his answer. He seemed to say something about it being his uncle's medal. Criss toyed with the medal in class but seemed content to leave it in his pocket as he headed out to the playground for recess. I later learned that his mother, grandmother, father, and brother had each told him that the medal could not be replaced if it got lost, but no one was sure if he really understood. According to his grandmother, who volunteers to help in his class from time to time, he finally stopped clutching the medal in his hands continuously as he had done before coming back to school."

Pull asked, "Do you think it was the same medal he had the day he took out the pervert who was trying to nab Betty Honda?"

"Yes, I think it was. The ribbon was dark blue with a broad, white strip in the middle and the medal was a bold cross," Mary responded.

Pull interrupted, "Mary, do you realize you were looking at the Navy Cross, the highest decoration that may be bestowed by the Navy Department?"

Mary answered, "No, I didn't have any idea how significant the medal is. But that explains why the medical technician was so impressed when he saw it. I wonder if Criss knows what the medal stands for. If so, his clutching it like he does might have a deeper meaning than we understand."

Pull said thoughtfully, "You are right, Mary; it just might trigger something in his mind when he is confronted by people he considers to be evil. It's fascinating stuff to think about, but let's get back to our conversation. Where was Billy and his gang when the ruckus started?"

"Relax Pull, I am getting there," Mary said sharply.

"Billy Benez, the kid the other kids call the Bully, was particularly obnoxious that day as he pushed his way around the playground. He was avoiding those he could not intimidate while cursing and indiscriminately calling people obscene names. He strutted along like a beast looking for someone to prey upon. I later learned that one of Billy's gangsters told him about this puny kid with a valuable-looking thing in his pocket. Billy must have thought it was his lucky day, because it has been said that he took off to find this kid like a racehorse at the starting gate. He evidently confronted Criss in the same bold manner he confronted other kids he considered inferior. Compared to Criss, Billy is a giant. He towers over him and every other kid on the playground. Billy had a way of intimidating kids by acting like he owned the playground and everything on it. I was later told by one of the gangsters that Billy demanded to see what Criss had in his pocket. It seemed to disturb Criss, but he didn't act as if he understood. Criss just ignored Billy."

"So, where were you in relation to Billy, Criss, and the others?" Pull inquired.

Mary continued as if she had not heard Pull's inquiry, "I knew what the playground had become and stayed pretty close to my special kids so I was able to see exactly what happened at that point. Billy, always mindful that his gang wanted to see some action, reached down and grabbed Criss's skinny arm so forcefully that the medal Criss was holding inside his pocket flew out. Criss suddenly realized what Billy wanted; he wanted his special medal. Billy, cursing at Criss, bent down to grab the medal. Criss's persona seemed to change as he straightened up like a soldier saluting. I suspect that a latent longing for justice welled up inside Criss. Anguish from the many insults and abuses he and others had endured at the hands of Billy and his gangsters may have boiled up to the surface. He looked fearless, and seemed like a new creature with a hyperactive adrenal gland. He was probably faced, for the first time in his life, with a flight or fight decision. When Billy grabbed his medal, the decision was made. Fight it would be. A surge of strength driven by a lifetime of pent-up emotion seemed to come over Criss."

"And then, without giving any apparent thought to it, Criss turned around and retreated about twenty feet. This gave Billy and his gang great satisfaction, judging from their laughs and shouts. They were probably thinking the skinny kid was going to do what skinny kids do; run away. As Billy stood gloating with the loot, Criss did a most peculiar thing. He turned to face Billy straight on, looked him square in the eyes—a very uncharacteristic gesture—and ran straight at him faster than I have ever seen a kid run. As Criss got within six feet of the startled and amused looking Billy, he jumped feet first into the air with his body parallel to the ground like an airborne human torpedo aimed right at Billy's chest. The sounds were loud and rapid; *slam—thud—scream*. It was a direct hit. Billy was knocked backward at least five feet. He was hit so hard that he just laid there. He was helpless, gasping for breath as splatterings of blood spewed forth with each breath exhaled."

Mary paused as if to catch her breath, and said, "I couldn't believe it. There was this giant of a kid, Billy, in obvious pain wallowing around in the dirt crying like a baby. He was unable to even plead for help."

Pull, totally caught up in the story, asked with an uncharacteristic excitement, "What about Billy's gang? What did they do?"

"His gang, and just about everyone else, including me, watched dumbfounded by what we had just witnessed. Criss, completely unharmed, calmly retrieved his medal, gave Billy a casual glimpse, and said a few unintelligible words in a stern voice directly to him. It sounded more like a command to a third person rather than anything else. He then walked away as if nothing had happened."

"Wow!" Pull interjected. "That must have been an astounding sight. What did you do then?"

"Well, Pull, I kept my composure, somewhat, and called 911 immediately. I then sought out Criss, thinking Billy's gang might mob him. As it turned out, that was not going to happen. No one dared to confront Criss, at least not right then. The gangsters were confused and scared like everyone else. The weak little kid had all of a sudden become a person to fear or respect, depending on your point of view. I had a sincere desire to protect Criss, but I was equally interested in confirming that he really did what I had just seen."

"Everyone else saw the same thing I did. We were all just kind of standing around with, I suspect, dumbfounded looks on our faces. It was unreal. It didn't take long for the story to get around the school campus and the entire community. As you might imagine, there were as many variations of the story as there were people to tell it. I truly wondered if I had seen a miracle. After thinking the situation over carefully, I concluded that the encounter I had just witnessed between 'Billy the Bully' and Criss had changed both of them, perhaps forever."

Mary said in a very thoughtful manner, "I have to admit, Pull, my mind buzzed with thoughts about handling this. It was the most dramatic sight I had ever seen in my entire life, and I think you know I have seen just about everything. This was like a David and Goliath thing. I knew people would be asking questions and, as you know, I feared some of them might be personal, too personal."

"Aha!" Pull exclaimed. "I can see why you were so reluctant to be interviewed. You were right, being an eyeball witness to an event that some would call miraculous makes you a prime candidate for all kinds of inquiries. Some snoopy reporter might go to extremes to get an insight on your involvement. Hey! I guess I am a good example of what a snoopy reporter can come up with, huh?" Pull said with his usual disarming smile.

Mary snickered and said, "Oh! You really are a clever dude. You know when to use sugar and when to use spice to get your story. You know something, I am glad, really glad even, that you forced me to get this out in the open. Perhaps Billy will tell you his take on it as well someday. I have already told Father Mark that you two helped me a great deal, and I know whatever I did in my past can't hold my mind in bondage any longer. I don't want to sound maudlin, but I know you burned a lot of calories digging into my background. Thanks for the effort."

Mary went on, "So, there you have it, Pull. I know you are trying to figure out how Criss did it, but I don't even have a good theory to lay on you, at least not a scientific theory. There certainly was something going on in Criss's brain which caused a physical reaction much more powerful than a super adrenal rush could produce. Also, the kind of ritualistic talk Criss did over the fallen body of his antagonist in each incident got me thinking about a spiritual dimension. You, no doubt, have read the stories in the *Megacity Times* about all of Criss's encounters, but perhaps

I should share what I know about them as well. If all you know, which I am sure it isn't, is what you read in that paper, you have a grossly distorted view."

Pull jumped at Mary's offer to share her observations by saying sincerely, "Thanks, Mary. You really are the best possible source for getting the facts; please continue. I am totally grateful and promise not to interrupt—very often."

Mary replied, "Pull, interrupt all you want. Isn't that your job? Here are the facts; at least as I know them. Billy was out of commission for a while after he felt the full force of Criss's wrath. A few days in the hospital followed by a few more days in juvenile detention left his gang leaderless. Just as I had feared, even without Billy's leadership, the gang felt the duty to avenge his humiliation. It seemed they fell into the usual gang mindset; if one member can't beat an opponent, then pile on until the entire gang is involved."

To which Pull replied, "You can't imagine how many times I have heard that story over the years."

Mary continued, "Oh yes, I can! Well, here is what happened. They set what they thought would be a trap for Criss, probably with encouragement from older gang members from their 'hood.' Criss was doing his usual running on the playground when a few gangsters stepped in front of him, forcing him to run between two gauntlet-like lines of gangsters. I later learned that the trap was carefully planned; some of them even had bicycle chains. They did not think he would stop running, but if he did, so much the better. They thought that they could beat him until someone in authority came, then they would scurry away like mice. I saw this developing but before I could react, Criss had wiped out six of them. Instead of running into the trap, he apparently sensed the danger and quickly darted around in a circle as the startled gangsters looked on. He launched himself, just as he had done with Billy, into the air. His torpedo-like body flew feet first, parallel to the ground for at least ten feet, knocking kids over like dominos.

When he landed, there were six kids moaning and crying on the ground with several others scattered across the playground. As for Criss, he paused and seemed to sternly utter a few words as he looked at each of the whimpering kids individually, and then continued to run as if nothing had happened."

"Did that silence the other gangsters?" Pull asked.

"No, it didn't. You would have thought those gang guys would have learned a lesson. But the old macho nonsense is a big motivator in the world of gangs. So, what did they do? They planned another assault. Mind you, this was without Billy urging them on. I learned later that he actually tried to persuade his friends to forget it, but that could not be done. This was war, a gang war. As I talked individually with the gang members afterward, I learned something about the dynamics of life in the gangs. Several of the younger boys said they did not want to hurt the 'crazy kid,' but they had to go along. None of them wanted to be ridiculed by the older guys they looked up to. It was now more than the honor of Billy; it was everybody in the 'hood' against this 'crazy kid.' It seems they just could not stand the thought of one little punk, as they put it, beating up the whole gang. The 'crazy kid' didn't fight the right way. He was supposed to get his friends to help."

Pull had covered many gang-related stories over the years and thought he knew how they operated. He still struggled with understanding the tangled thinking which caused otherwise healthy young boys to do such mindless things. He thought Mary could provide some insight when he asked her, "Do you have any idea why these kids do, at times, act like savages?"

Mary replied, "It is an acceptance thing coupled with peer pressure. All people have a desire to belong, to fit in. Our culture offers young people many wholesome opportunities to satisfy that basic need. Think for a moment about a high school football team as an example of acceptable gang behavior. Players wear special colors, and they have a mascot which sets them apart from other teams—or 'gangs.' But most importantly, the team offers a sense of belonging and a chance for recognition. Unfortunately, many of these kids at this level are under the control of big brothers, cousins, and even parents that, for whatever reason, are not comfortable with socially acceptable alternatives to gang involvement. Projecting an image of being anti-social brings 'respect' in the 'hood.' The older kids are, in many instances, compelled by a perverted sense of honor and duty to coerce the younger ones into joining street gangs by old-fashioned peer pressure. This kind of thing can really get nasty. Getting back to your question, a young boy can be conditioned to suppress his own individual conscience, and accept brutality as the price of admission to a gang. The big boys don't fight with just fists and feet; they fight with chains, knives, and guns. Anything goes when honor is at stake. I remember so well just how brutal it can get from my own experiences as a kid."

Pull responded, "I never thought of it that way."

Then he asked, "How is all this turmoil going over with the other kids at Moreville?"

Mary answered, "I sensed tensions were getting high around the community. Older guys from 'the hood' were beginning to cruise by school, ostensibly to drop off or pick up their brothers, cousins, or friends. By that time, it looked like Jimmie More and those he hung out with were beginning to feel challenged, agitated, and perhaps fearful. Pull, surely you must have read the police reports?"

"Yes, I did, Mary. The police reports I read indicated that the older gang bangers admitted they wanted to raise the level of anxiety. One of the hard-core gang bangers was quoted as saying, 'A riot would have played right into our hands.' I know from jogging downtown that there are a lot of store fronts on Main Street that would be easy to knock off."

Mary interjected, "It seems hard-core gangsters often brag about knowing the fine art of manipulating and agitating for the purpose of starting a lucrative free-for-all. After all, the ACLA can usually be counted on to provide legal cover, having repeatedly tried to make the claim that these people are downtrodden minorities just taking back what someone took from their ancestors a long time ago."

This was a disturbing thought to Pull. "It looks like a race riot can be managed like a business with little or no consequence for those who might get busted," he said to Mary with a thick tone of disgust.

"Pull," Mary said. "It is worse than you think. Experts in criminology have told me that this knowledge is easily acquired at the Megacity Jail, the 'college of crime' as some derisively call it. They call it Gang Management 101. With my background and training, I am sensitive to these issues and know how fast a small incident can get out of control. I did everything I could to warn the administration that serious trouble was brewing. Mr. Noe Itall, our principal, was unimpressed, and cautioned against being judgmental. Finally, your friend Captain Studly stepped in and essentially demanded that Noe Itall prepare a plan to protect the students in case of a riot. Principal Noe Itall let it be known that insurrections were not his responsibility, but he did agree to appoint a committee to study the problem."

"What?" Pull exclaimed. "The police were concerned about a possible riot and the principal wants to appoint a committee?"

Mary paused, looked at Pull with a frown, and said, "Come on! Don't act like you don't believe me. You know that guy. He is a spineless tower of jelly completely subservient to forces behind the scene."

"Ouch!" Pull thought. "This little lady is more perceptive than I realized. She sure has the man figured out."

Then she continued, "I was present at the school board meeting when they wisely asked Captain Studly for advice. His first bit of advice was to establish a twenty-four-seven graffiti removal squad in conjunction with the city to discourage taggers before they made a habit of tagging Moreville, and then to install a six-foot-high chain-link fence completely around the playground. Further, he advised closely monitoring entry to the school. The school board instructed Noe Itall to follow the Captain's suggestions, but Itall thought other suggestions should be heard first because he did not want to alienate any group or sub-group in our rapidly diversifying community. Noe Itall was told he could meet all he wanted and talk all he wanted, but the school was moving out on Studly's advice. The big, ugly fence—which we both know so well—surrounding the playground was installed within a week, much to the chagrin of some long-time residents. It just was not the Moreville way."

Mary continued relating what she heard at the school board meeting. "Noe Itall reported that his ad hoc committee urged adopting a suggestion advocated by the ACLA to placate the gang by expelling Criss. He argued that surely the minority group would see a victory and back off. Many civic leaders were so irate by Noe Itall's suggestion, that they pressed the school board to buy out his contract and send him packing."

As Pull listened to Mary, he simultaneously posted on his blog, "In a way, I was amused by the thought of a puny little kid like Criss beating up the gang single-handedly. As I listened to Mary Gonzales lecture me like a student in one of her classes, I could not help but wonder why these gang bangers could not see how cowardly they really were. The bravado and manufactured macho looked like a screen to hide their insecurity. This elementary school feud was on the verge of becoming a race riot. It was irrational, utterly irrational."

Mary said, "I had great concern that trouble was brewing because word coming my way from the 'hood' indicated that the gangsters, who were always influenced by hard-core ex-jail birds, were talking about bigger things. They laid low but not because they had backed off, as Noe Itall predicted. Strangely enough, Billy Benez urged his followers to back off as well, putting himself at risk in doing so. If there are any cooler heads in situations like that they are the ones who lay low. The 'don't just get even, get ahead' code of the street had to be obeyed."

Mary shaking her head in disgust added, "It is pathetic to see these kids being manipulated. It is common knowledge in the law enforcement community that older gangsters are too sophisticated to care about the 'code.' They had other things in mind. The 'code' was nothing but a motivator for the young ones who were eager to prove themselves. According to jailhouse wisdom, this situation had the potential of developing into a profitable race riot. These thugs no doubt thought it would be great training for the young bloods."

Pull added, "Mary, you are right about high-level gang involvement. I have seen all the police reports. They document how interrogations revealed a plan to do a home invasion at the Crosswauld's. The plan was abandoned because the gang's drive-by surveillances revealed that the target home had all kinds of security, which could only be seen by 'experienced,' older gangsters. The gangsters were convinced that a patrol car rolled on Crosswauld's street every ten minutes. The leaders concluded that the likelihood of getting busted for what might be considered a felony was greater than the gain, even if they looted the place."

Mary jumped in saying, "We probably read the same reports. I have to say, I was shocked when I learned that police investigations uncovered some unknown details about local gang activity."

She continued, "Here is a little insight from my own experience that you won't find in a police report. Billy Benez returned to school a different kid after his confrontation with Criss. His attitude had changed, and he waited for me to arrive at school one morning. He was very disturbed and looked frightened as he asked in a whisper if he could talk to me secretly. After we slipped into a nearby vacant office, he said he did not want any more trouble at school but was afraid he would be blamed for something his friends were planning to do. Naturally, I pressed him hard to learn what was going on. After a lot of hemming and hawing, he finally said he heard a guy he and the others looked up to, say he wanted to tell them what being a real gangster was all about. He told them how they had to do stuff to earn respect and said, 'The little b-d deserved to be hurt, hurt bad. If you guys shoot him, everyone will know you have what it takes to get respect.' Then this guy said, 'It would teach all those Moreville people a lesson and, at the same time, it'd be a great initiation for guys who want to get in good with us.' He had everyone excited and was laughing as he said, 'Something like that just might cause retaliation, maybe even a race riot. This could be fun.' Other students began to glance our way as Billy and I hovered in a corner, so Billy made a hasty departure before he finished telling me what he had on his mind."

Mary continued, "By this time, I had developed a good relationship with Billy. The occasional visits to Helen's Heavenly Hamburger might have helped, so I fully expected he would want to talk again soon. At this point, I began to realize that I was probably the only adult in his life he could trust. That same day he slipped me a crudely written note asking to talk. I arranged for Billy to be called into the vice principal's office ostensibly for discipline. He told us, 'Look, I don't like ratting out my friends, and I don't like that kid who clobbered me, but I don't want to kill him. I am going to tell you what I know. If anything happens, don't blame me. They are planning to kill him, or at least shoot him.' Billy went on to say, 'An older guy had a neat, little gun he said he used for small jobs and offered it to anyone who was tough enough to use it. About five or six Moreville El guys eagerly shouted that they would do it. A hand-off was made to one of my guys with a few words about how to load, shoot, and handle the gun. The guy who owned the gun told everyone to be cool and not to worry. He said that if we are really close, we couldn't miss hitting him. He also said that we will get away with it because we are kids, and nobody will be able to prove who actually pulled the trigger. He told everyone that the police will ask each of us who did it and try to scare us, but just to say we don't know and stick with that story. He told us that we will all be really big on the street after it is over.'"

Pull was taken aback by the thought of such a cold-blooded deed being committed by these youngsters. He shared with Mary what he had read in the police report about this same incident. The police report read, "The school administration notified the department immediately after learning of a possible plot to harm Criss, but the school took no precautions to protect him." Also in the report, Principal Noe Itall stated to the investigator, "We don't know if the Benez kid's story is true. It may be an exaggeration of the facts. It is probably just young people trying to act tough with no real intentions to harm anyone. There is really nothing we can do. As long as the Crosswauld kid is part of our student body there will probably be some kind of trouble."

"Mary, that is your principal they are quoting there," Pull said in exasperation.

"Oh, I know, Pull. Why don't you take him back East with you when you go?"

A few days after the possible threat to Criss was reported, police were called to the campus to investigate a crime which shook Moreville. According to the police report, "Five young, Moreville El students, armed with a small caliber handgun, casually walked into the special education area after being dropped off early at the school by an unidentified car. Under individual questioning, they revealed that they planned to ambush Criss with deadly force."

The report went on, "Unbeknownst to anyone but the suspects, the alleged target, Criss Crosswauld, walked across the campus heading for a trap that had been carefully thought out. As Crosswauld approached, a lookout for the would-be shooter slowly opened a door to a maintenance closet. Inside, awaited the rest of the suspects. The lookout peeked out to see Crosswauld approaching. Before the lookout could give a prearranged signal, it is believed that Crosswauld instinctively knew there was danger and quickly responded with a maneuver he had not used in prior incidents. Crosswauld jumped straight up and turned with his foot extended so forcefully against the door that the lookout's head was briefly caught in a vise-like grip. As the lookout screamed and fell to the floor, the remaining suspects emerged through the door and attempted to flee the scene. The suspects trampled over their fallen comrade only to be gutted by a spinning dynamo. The suspects either fell or were knocked to the floor one by one as they fled. The last one out, still dressed in his unseasonably heavy coat to hide the gun which he gripped in a deep pocket, felt Crosswauld's strength like no other. A small foot at the end of a skinny leg landed chest high with such impact that the other suspects said it sounded 'like a wrecking ball hitting the side of a building.' The gun discharged as the suspect struggled to get it out of his pocket before the dynamo hit, slightly wounding himself."

Mary quickly added, "I read that report too. I guess it came from interrogation of the gangsters. You would not believe what I experienced. I was just outside the room when I heard the shot. Scared of what I might find, I rushed into the room. I was anxious, out of breath, and prepared for anything other than what I saw. It was unbelievable. Four kids, every one of them much bigger than Criss, were cowering in a corner, some crying. Flat on the floor, bleeding slightly, was the would-be shooter. He had a gun partly protruding from his coat pocket. Again, I sounded the emergency alarm and turned to look for Criss. Since he was out of sight, I feared that he had been harmed. To my relief, I found him down on his knees crouched behind my desk picking a book off the bookshelf. Again, he acted as if nothing had happened. I asked the gangster kids what happened and each said the same thing. 'That crazy kid scared us the way he acted after knocking us down,' they all said. 'He came to each of us and stared with mean eyes and said, 'Get out.' Then he disappeared. It was really weird.'"

Pull, shaking his head as if in disbelief, almost shouted as he exclaimed, "Mary, if I did not know you like I do, I would find that unbelievable. It is no wonder Criss has so many admirers."

Pull again thanked her for her courage and candor. "It is by far the most complete account yet of the events which make Criss a superhero. It really puts everything in a different light. I am going to go back and reread the *Megacity Times* accounts of this and the other incidents. As I recall, the reporter, Nancy Malaprop, called all of Criss's encounters hate crimes perpetrated by an out-of-control, judo-trained, drug-crazed kid."

CHAPTER 10

The Noe Itall Hearing

The decision was made. Something had to be done about Criss Crosswauld, but what? On the one hand, all agreed—well, almost all—that Criss lived in a loving, nurturing home and received daily guidance at the best available special education facility. What more could be done for him? On the other hand, no less than twelve people had been attacked by Criss, one of them on a public sidewalk, giving the appearance to some observers that he was a threat to society and should be put away.

A semi-public meeting was held by the school. It was Noe Itall, the progressive, Congo-born principal at Moreville Elementary School, who came up with a solution. His solution was entirely consistent with his desire to be politically correct above all else. The solution had the added advantage of setting up an elaborate pretense for taking action, but with no real intent to drive to a decision. A decision, any real decision, would surely alienate one side or the other with the resultant ill will and possibly bad press. Itall was a master at such tactics; after all, he did keep the PTA, teacher's union, and school board placated by reorganizing the rather large staff at Moreville El every time there was a hint of dissatisfaction. He was confident that those who shared his elitist worldview would consider the proposal he was going to make brilliant. He had carefully planted suggestions that he would be interested in an appropriately high political office and was eager to participate in public debates as long as there was opportunity for talking and not much debating. He whispered to a group of supporters, "Hey, maybe I can turn this disagreeable situation into something favorable. My objective evenhandedness will surely be loved by all. A new career in politics just might open up. The opinion molders will demand that I serve a much broader segment of the populace which, of course, would include Megacity." His confidence seemed to soar when an exuberant ACLA confidant blurted out to no one in particular, "A clear precedent has been established. Mr. Noe Itall, you could go all the way to the U.S. Senate, maybe even the White House."

So it began. Noe Itall called a carefully planned press conference in which everybody that was anybody in the news dispensing business was invited, including a horde of bloggers of all political stripes. He prepared a lengthy speech with hard copies distributed to all attendees, which included Pull. Of course, Internet sources were included in the distribution so those who were in the ACLA camp could easily redistribute it without giving much thought to what was being said.

The speech was given in an eloquent manner. He paused appropriately and gestured to embellish his "profound" comments which he apparently thought demonstrated that he, more than any other human being, understood both sides of the question. He concluded his "Noe Itall" show by offering himself as an impartial chairman at an informal hearing board meeting. It would be a hearing with no binding legal authority. Instead, Noe Itall emphasized, "It would be a search for truth and compromise."

Noe Itall suggested that each side pick a speaker to represent his or her point of view. Naturally, all individuals desiring to speak would be given ample opportunity to do so before the hearing closed.

As Noe Itall spoke, he seemed pleased to see the beaming face of Hillary Cheatalot. She had reason to beam since she was more than likely hearing her own words coming from Noe Itall.

Noe Itall's smooth presentation all but assured his public hearing suggestion would be accepted by all concerned. Indeed, his hearing suggestion was accepted; it had to be. The *Megacity Times* front page coverage, and many in the legion of bloggers now tracking the story, presented the hearing idea as if it were a done deal. There really weren't any alternatives, except to do nothing, which Criss's supporters urged.

The "Imprison Criss Crosswauld" side, orchestrated by Hillary Cheatalot, had their spokesperson in mind before Noe Itall made his pitch. Nancy P. Malaprop—the *Megacity Times* expert on Moreville, the school, and particularly Criss Crosswauld—was chosen. She could lay claim to being the only objective reporter to cover all of Criss Crosswauld's altercations.

The "Keep Criss Free" side struggled with who should be the principal speaker. The whole idea of such a hearing smacked of a kangaroo court. There was Adam Crosswauld, Mary Gonzales, and several others to consider; all perfectly capable. But since the other side had picked a reporter, Pull Itzer's name came up as a logical choice. Pull did not consider himself an orator. He was a reporter who was accustomed to delivering the hard facts without opinion, except when his opinion was carefully delineated. He rejected the suggestion out of hand but dutifully reported on his Web site that the suggestion had been made.

That was it. A deluge of online followers and Bennie's Deli patrons responded with a "Go Itzer" campaign. It was settled, the possible fate of Criss would be determined by a Nancy P. Malaprop vs. Pull Itzer show-and-tell.

Pull knew about Malaprop's history of smoking exotic tobacco and other mind-altering substances. He wondered if she could stay sober long enough to do the job Cheatalot would expect.

Pull had a good idea of what the end game was for Cheatalot and he suspected the whole idea was hers from the start. As he saw it, she had a primary and a secondary goal. First, she wanted the hearing to help her pending lawsuit against Crosswauld et al. A misstatement or innuendo could be used in her lawsuit against those she claimed were liable for the damages done physically and psychologically to her clients. She referred to those clients as the "twelve victims of Criss." The defendants were the Crosswaulds, the Moreville School District, the judo instructor, the medical professional who prescribed Criss's medication, and the pharmaceutical company who produced the medication. Pull knew that pockets this deep could make a lawyer like Cheatalot salivate. The secondary objective was to destroy the Crosswaulds just because she could.

Cheatalot could not have had a lot of confidence in her personal selection. The only thing sloppier than Malaprop's personal appearance was her sloppy reporting, but Malaprop would have to do. The people trusted what they read in the newspaper. That was the American way, Ms. Cheatalot had probably reasoned. Besides, it was so obvious to her that the kid was a menace that anyone could carry the day. Cheatalot knew it would take some coaching to bring this willing idiot up to speed, but with the help of her pseudo-intellectual friends in the ACLA, it could be done. She had a well-known reputation among her intimate friends for holding the "Moreville crowd" in low regard. Naturally, she would enlist the help of her ACLA friends in the speech preparation and conditioning of Nancy P. Malaprop.

It was late in the evening of a very long day as Pull sat, squirreled away at his makeshift communications center in the corner of his hotel room, posting his latest blog while simultaneously scanning the huge backlog of e-messages. The thought of speaking on behalf of Criss and his supporters competed for his attention the way tight leg muscles compete with his desire to begin his morning jogging routine. He had to admit to himself that he was apprehensive, almost to the point of tormenting himself with the fear that he might not be up to the task of giving the kid the top-notch representation he deserved. "Heck!" he thought. "I have never considered myself to be a good public speaker. I didn't even like giving those lectures when I was teaching at the university. What have I gotten myself into?"

Then he noticed an e-message that begged for closer reading as he scanned hurriedly through the messages. It was from a frequent commenter who had previously remained anonymous. The message read:

> To Pull, my old friend from our days together in the newsroom. I have followed your blogs and commentary on the Moreville kid, Criss Cross. You're on the right side this time. That may sound strange coming from me, the guy who always took the liberal side of every position in the old days. Don't get me wrong, I haven't flipped. I have just learned that every issue doesn't have to be approached from an ideological point of view, and that ideology should never trump the truth. I still pay my dues to the Party. After all, it is how I stay employed in this jungle we call a city, and it gives me access to information that I would not otherwise have. So, here is the point, old buddy. I just attended an invitation-only meeting called by Hillary Cheatalot to brief Nancy Malaprop on the face-off you two are going to have. Hillary has always been edgy, but it looks like she has grown from a common ideologue to a dangerous activist completely devoid of honor or fairness. I took notes at the meeting and, of course, I had my trusty recorder blazing away so I would not be overly conspicuous. Here is the essence of what went on.
>
> Hillary Cheatalot was in rare form as the small group gathered to counsel Malaprop. She started out saying,

'Look, people, I want you to know right up front that I think the Crosswauld family should trade that kid in for a new one. They are really the villains here for not aborting the little bugger.' That little comment caused some in the small gathering to yell out, 'Hear, Hear,' while others laughed and others sat silently.

Hillary continued in the same vein, 'He is worthless and a burden on the rest of us. He is sucking up the oxygen in the air and creating an ever-increasing carbon footprint. Oh well, our society has not progressed to the point where the right thing could be done for the good of all. But with all of us working together, along with our friends in the media, the intelligentsia, and the judiciary, we will get there one day.'

This quote from Hillary will tell you a bit about her strategy. 'By the way, Nancy, you are not to even hint at expressing anything like what I just said. You have to play the goodness and light game. Remember, you will be fighting for the proletariat with every word you utter.'

Hillary went on to say, 'OK, people, what do we have on the Crosswauld family?' A slight, effeminate looking young man with a Middle Eastern appearance and a pronounced lisp stood up and said, 'I think I have something for background info. It probably would not be good material for Nancy's speech though. You know, we have all been puzzled by that Hitlerian-sounding name, Crosswauld. Well, I found that Criss Crosswauld's uncle was a notorious government agent. During my search of the public records and other places that I will not mention, I came across several citations given to one Jack (Jocko) Crosswauld. The citations were given to him to justify his war medals. Here is an example, *Crosswauld, while defending his subordinates who were under heavy fire from enemy combatants, counter charged, killing fifteen of the enemy combatants*—bla, bla, bla. There you have it; anyone who reads reputable newspapers and journals knows that the term 'enemy combatants' is a right-wing code for innocent civilians. Furthermore, Crosswauld was killed by a bomb; but guess what? I have it from a reliable insider source that he was an expert bomb maker and had a huge bomb stored in his own car. As he drove into his own driveway with his family, the darn thing went off killing the lot of them.'

I became increasingly bothered by the nature of the meeting. Consider this statement Hillary excitedly made, 'That's good info, but, Nancy, if you touch on this aspect of the Crosswauld family, don't emphasize the medal stuff. Most of these backward, redneck people still think such uncivilized, murderous behavior is somehow justified and right. Oh, when will they ever learn? Again, Nancy, be strong and don't forget you are fighting for a cause bigger than any one person, so go for it with all you have.'

Nancy Malaprop seemed so charged up that her head must have been spinning. She acted like she had just won an award. She said to no one in particular, 'I am ready. I will be on all the TV channels, not as a small-time, obscure reporter, but as a spokesperson for a cause bigger than any one person.' She continued to babble to anyone and everyone about what a great opportunity she will have to show all 'those jerks' (I guess that would be you and me, pal) who have criticized her over the years. I heard her say, 'Oh, I can hardly wait.'

Pull rarely had time to respond to e-messages, but this time he did so with great enthusiasm. He expressed gratitude to his old friend, now informant, for providing insight as to the mindset of Hillary Cheatalot and her associates. He also thanked him for giving him a "heads-up" on what to expect from Nancy Malaprop.

Pull invited his friend to join him for coffee, conversation, and bagels at Bennie's Deli after things settled down. Given what Pull knew about the circumstances surrounding Jocko's death, the guy who told the distorted version seemed sinister. Pull, always the investigative reporter, felt duty-bound to see if his friend could, or would, reveal a little about this guy's background.

This unexpected e-message invigorated Pull, causing his anxiety to give way to an adrenaline rush as he speculated about why the stuff about Jocko was even brought up. There surely was more to this whole deal than he could have imagined that evening at the Studly's when he jumped on the campaign to defend Criss—a campaign which had been orchestrated by Aggie. He could not remember exactly what it was that motivated him to burn so much energy; intuition, or perhaps a touch of providence, drew him into this tangled story. He did not know the reason, but he knew for sure that there were a lot more rocks to look under.

Criss was sort of a folk hero. A cross section of folks came forward to offer Pull support as the hearing date approached. The entire Criss Cross Defense Team offered much advice on the matter. He had the facts, and he was fired up after reading his friend's e-message. Pull wanted moral support and prayers from those so inclined. He received both in abundance as he attended a private get-together held at the More mansion the night before the big hearing. All the long-time supporters were there; Aggie, Mary and her husband, all the Crosswaulds, Slip Knott, the Studlys, the entire More family, and countless others. It seemed most of the student body at Moreville El wanted to attend, but only a few of Jimmie's friends were invited. It was a meaningful experience for Pull. He had never before felt such solidarity. He was surprised and pleased to see Aggie, smiling discreetly in her alluring manner. "How did she know about this meeting? Does this amazing woman know how I feel about her?" His thoughts were a temporary, but pleasant distraction.

The order of speech was determined by lot with Nancy P. Malaprop speaking first. Naturally, Mr. Noe Itall had a few appropriate words to kick off the event. His self-aggrandizing comments were what the folks in Moreville had come to expect from him. Few were impressed by his attempt to paint a picture of sacrifice to the community for having given them the gift of his considerable skills in moderating this event. Some folks were so rude as to express publicly that they thought it was his duty, not a special sacrifice.

"Both sides coming together like this in a spirit of compromise and reconciliation surely will be a historical high-water mark for our fine community as we struggle together to fight the evils of discrimination, bigotry, and overt aggressiveness," droned Noe Itall. The crowd was getting impatient, many of whom had just about had enough of this "master at talking without saying anything."

Finally, Noe Itall introduced the first speaker as being the most informed person on the subject of Criss Crosswauld's behavior. "She established her credentials by objectively reporting on every altercation Crosswauld had on or near the campus while working as a reporter for the prestigious *Megacity Times,"* he said.

Nancy P. Malaprop was attired in a fashionable but conservative suit, her hair was done up to look like a Hollywood celebrity. She looked more professional than anyone could remember her looking in the past. She cautiously climbed the elevated platform that had hastily been erected at the high school football stadium. It was the only place in town big enough to hold the expected crowd.

Pull noticed that she appeared to be a little wobbly, and her eyes looked sleepy. He thought to himself with a grin on his face, "She may have just lost her balance. On the other hand, she may need a drink to get through this. She does not have the truth on her side, and she knows it. That would make even someone as tough as Hillary nervous, and she is not anywhere near that tough."

Malaprop began, "Thank you, Mr. Chairman. You have indeed done an outstanding job putting this all together. I know the community is indebted to you and thanks you as citizens of Moreville and the world. I am honored and particularly well qualified to represent the side of this dispute that fears for the safety of our children should Criss Crosswauld be allowed to remain among us. This is a law-abiding community, and he is a public nuisance that should be put in a place where he cannot hurt himself or anyone else. I know that may sound like a harsh thing to say. I am prepared to say harsh things today, however, because I love this community and will face any obstacle to keep it safe for the children. Moreville Elementary School has been rendered unsafe, in spite of the best efforts of Mr. Noe Itall. I speak with authority on this matter. I have been the first objective reporter on the scene at each of the three significant altercations Criss Crosswauld has had with his fellow students. I, of course, was there when the unfortunate, downtrodden man was mauled on the public sidewalk in front of the school. There have been no less than twelve innocent victims of his aggression so far. How many more will we tolerate before taking action? I repeat, he is a menace who must be stopped. I have recorded that his attacks have gotten progressively more brutal. He destroyed the new fence at Moreville El to get at a poor fellow walking on the sidewalk. I don't deal in rumors, but you should be aware that there are widely circulated stories on the Internet that pretty well confirm other reports which indicate the altercations I first reported on may just be the tip of the iceberg."

"There might have been many other unreported incidents, suppressed by someone sympathetic to vigilante behavior in law enforcement. Manic-depressive sufferers can explode with anger and great strength unexpectedly. Their behavior is unpredictable and erratic. Such behavior is bad at best, but when the manic-depressive is judo-trained and is taking methamphetamines, anything can happen. Criss Crosswauld may look like a sweet, harmless kid but he is anything but harmless. Our children are not safe with him around. That isn't all, there is another dimension to this deplorable situation that we should keep in mind. The ugly face of racism was present in each of the altercations I have reported on, except the hapless fellow mauled out on the sidewalk, and he likely was mistaken for a minority because of his heavy beard. My considerable experience as a journalist has taught me to recognize hate crimes when I see them."

Pull sat relaxed and smiling as he whispered to a companion sitting next to him, "She has lost it. If her voice gets any shriller, the folks on the front row may be bailing out anytime now."

Malaprop went on, "Look at the evidence. Every one of the victims was a Hispanic student timidly trying to assimilate into a new environment. In every case, they were slammed brutally in the body with a lethal weapon, Crosswauld's feet. This powerful judo-trained bigot used excessive force, which is common in hate crimes. Also note that several of the victims were hospitalized and have no doubt been traumatized by his brutal assault. Many, I suspect, will suffer life-long mental anguish."

"Yes, I know some of you seem to like what Crosswauld has done. Some even think he is a hero. But thinking he is a hero does not make him one, nor does it give him the right to be a vigilante. A real hero would bring his grievances to the attention of enlightened authorities like Mr. Noe Itall."

"As to the frequent claim that Crosswauld's family is loving and nurturing, I remind you that so is the family of the wildest of animals. You might be disturbed, as I was, to learn that this poor kid has been forced to attend a bigoted church almost every Sunday of his life. He attends a church that preaches a doctrine of strict exclusion. They claim their way is the only way."

"A true model of loving and nurturing is the family who teaches turning the other cheek, unconditional acceptance of different people and different cultures, and peaceful coexistence with all the people of the world. This whole nasty episode could have been avoided if the Crosswauld family had truly been loving and nurturing by seeing that he received proper sensitivity training from his earliest days. Instead, I fear they inculcated him with concepts of extreme nationalism, which in turn brought about war worship and a sense of supremacy of one group of people over another. That is the foundation of all hate crimes."

"Another little bit of information you might find interesting is that this boy's uncle was a trained killer who worked for the government until he blew himself and his family up with a home-made bomb."

"I leave you with this final thought. We all must live within the law and do all that we can to discourage those who would engage in renegade endeavors. The best possible thing that can be done for this most unfortunate child would be to liberate him from his unenlightened parents and place him in a state-managed facility for children with neurological disorders, manic-depressive behavior, or whatever it is that makes him do such vicious things to his fellow man. I suggest to you, Mr. Chairman, and fellow citizens of Moreville, that we must protect the children at all cost. Thank you."

Malaprop frequently glanced at Cheatalot at the beginning of her speech, who was strategically located in the front row as planned. They both thought that non-verbal communications would be helpful. Malaprop got carried away with the message's delivery and did not pay attention to Cheatalot, a mistake that could be costly. Had she been watching her mentor, she would have noticed a change in demeanor from smugness to dejection as the speech progressed.

Departing the speaker's platform immediately as if she had not considered that there may be a question and answer period, the beaming Malaprop seemed to be pleased with her performance. Perhaps she was thinking she had delivered a powerful message, maybe a knockout punch. Then she caught the stare, the ice-cold stare of a stoic Hillary Cheatalot.

She must have thought, "What gives here? I may have over-reached, but I hit all the talking points. What does it take to make that woman smile? Anyway, those camera dudes are taking lots of pictures, which must have made Cheatalot happy. I have made it. Who knows what the future may bring?"

Chairman Noe Itall thanked Ms. Malaprop for her insightfulness. Then he started to introduce Pull Itzer, paused, shuffled a few sheets of paper, and got a look of shock on his face that was hard to hide. Somebody had let him down. There wasn't a prepared intro for him to read. After all the bragging he had done about his skills as a moderator, this was a little embarrassing. Pull, noticing the mishap, thought to himself, "His administrative assistant will catch it for this." Being a great speech reader didn't help Noe Itall, he had to do the intro off the cuff. He mumbled a few unintelligible words and finally said, "I really don't know the gentleman who will be speaking on behalf of the status quo. I believe he is a recent visitor who gained some experience as a reporter for a reputable newspaper in the East. It is my understanding that he is no longer employed in that capacity. I have been told he is in Moreville to cover the unusual circumstances surrounding Criss Crosswauld." Itall went on to say, "I thought it was somewhat unusual that those on the status quo side of this issue chose an outsider." Quickly adding, "However, it was their right to do so, and I urge tolerance and compassion if the gentleman does not quite understand the complexities of life in a suburb-like Moreville. Perhaps, Mr. Pull Itzer, you can fill us in?"

Pull chuckled to himself as he took the podium thinking, "What a pretentious putz this guy Itall is. People all over the world follow my blog, and he does not know anything about me. Maybe he should talk to some of his own students."

Pull scanned the crowd, smiling broadly to his many friends, especially to the T-shirt clad kids scattered throughout the large crowd. Then he said with an even bigger smile, "I gotta get one of those T-shirts." The crowd roared its approval. Noe Itall pounded the table to get order.

Pull spoke up, "The chairman is absolutely right. We have to maintain proper decorum. We can celebrate afterwards. I'll buy the first dozen pizzas," prompting another roar from students and adults alike. "Bennie Delivers!" shouted a jovial fellow in the back of the crowd, prompting good-natured laughs.

With that, Pull raised his hands with his palms facing the crowd. He resembled a president giving a State of the Union Address and said, "Thank you, thank you, thank you." Pull was also pleased that he saw Billy Benez sitting with Mr. and Mrs. Gonzales right down on the front row.

Clearing his throat, Pull nodded appropriately toward the chairman and his opponent and said, "Thank you, Mr. Chairman and my worthy opponent, Ms. Malaprop. And thank you, my newfound friends, the citizens of Moreville." Again, more than a smattering of applause came from the suddenly energized crowd.

"It is true, I am a newcomer here. I assure you, however, that the ethical requirements of my proud profession require me to do thorough research before commenting on any subject. The chairman's introduction suggested that I came here to Moreville as an unemployed reporter in search of a story. That is partly true. I did leave the East Coast news machine where I worked. Many of you may know it as the one that is celebrated for printing all the news that fits. It was falling apart and may be on its deathbed. And yes, I came looking for a story. That is what newsmen do. When I first arrived here in Moreville, getting the story and getting it right was my only objective; but I admit that the more I have learned about the Crosswauld family, the more I have come to respect and admire them. Few families have sacrificed so much and yet have been subjected to such harsh treatment."

"I stand here today not as a reporter, but as an advocate of this good and decent kid who has been blessed with a fine family and extraordinary physical strength. I have read every by-line that Ms. Malaprop has written, and listened carefully to her remarks here today. I must say, had Ms. Malaprop been my student during my brief tenure as a journalism professor, I would have urged her to seek employment in another field." Again, widespread laughter and giggling could be heard from the crowd.

Noe Itall quickly pounded the table and pleaded with the restless crowd to be calm and listen to all sides without prejudice. As Noe Itall tried to control the crowd, he became uneasy. He almost lost his composure as he looked across a sea of kids, his students in large measure, wearing crazily designed shirts that read, "**Criss Cross Saves**" and "**Leave Criss Alone**" and "**Free Criss**." Noe Itall had seen, and as a young community organizer, had led many demonstrations, but these troublemakers seemed to be protesting him. It was enough to cause a budding politician to rethink launching a career in politics in Moreville.

Pull continued, "We are gathered here to talk about Criss Cross and what should be done, if anything, about him. So, let me tell you about Criss. But first, I want to clarify an important point. There is no scientific research supporting the claim that there is a relationship between autism and manic depression as the previous speaker implied."

"I have had the pleasure of visiting with Criss's family on several occasions, even breaking bread together a few times. I can tell you that this young man is beyond remarkable in certain areas. On one occasion, I was chatting with the family while the History Channel was playing an episode about Thomas Jefferson's life in the background. The actor playing Jefferson gave an emotional reading of the Declaration of Independence, which I did not pay much attention to nor did anyone else, or so I thought. I asked

Jack, Criss's brother, what the program was about, just making small talk. Jack turned to Criss sitting on the floor beside him and said, 'Tell Mr. Itzer what we just heard.' With that, Criss stood up and recited the entire Declaration of Independence, just as the actor had done; even with the same inflection and timing. I was flabbergasted. Adam, Criss's dad, told me, 'He does stuff like that often, sometimes remembering the whole script of a character in a TV production. We encourage him to do things like that, but never question what he understands.'"

"It is true, as the previous speaker said; Criss's parents do take him to the church of their choice. Isn't that what we believe in this country when we talk about freedom of religion? And isn't it the parents' right and responsibility to train children to be righteous and to follow in their footsteps? This is still America, isn't it?" Many shouts of "amen" could be heard from the otherwise silent crowd.

"I think we can all agree that Criss has done some remarkable things. I am also confident that many of us join with countless Internet followers of Criss in asking, 'How does he do it?' I have been on a personal quest to shed light on that question. I am not prepared to rule out the strong possibility that a critical factor in the answer to that question can be found in the lessons learned during those church services. The same services the previous speaker spoke of so derisively. The answer to the 'how' question remains elusive, but can anyone deny the possibility that the 'why' question can be answered in his following of a moral compass?" The repeated shouts of "amen" were now augmented by thunderous applause.

"Now, let's get down to the facts pertaining to Criss's alleged attacks on innocent people. Let's take them chronologically, starting with the most recent and most spectacular incident. Are you aware that the guy Criss allegedly smashed, I say allegedly because the police report indicates that no one came forth with a positive identification on Criss, was a convicted molester with a long criminal record? He is now awaiting trial and no doubt will be off the streets for a long time. Most of you know what happened. But a general recap might be helpful. Criss heard the scream of a fellow student on the sidewalk who was being accosted by this evil person. Somehow, Criss broke through the fence and rescued the student. Her name is Betty Honda, and she is here with us today with her parents. In the process of rescuing Betty, Criss somehow caused the criminal to fly up on the hood of his automobile, thereby preventing an escape. It would have been hard to escape anyway, since the bad guy was gasping for air and unable to go anywhere under his own power. Try telling the Honda family that Criss is not a hero, and that he is a menace to society." The audience broke out in loud, spontaneous applause and shouts of support for Criss. Again, Noe Itall called for the audience to use more restraint when such emotional statements are made.

"Now, let's review the episodes before Criss apprehended the molester. Did you know that your police department successfully headed off a planned home invasion of the Crosswauld's home by older, hardened members of the same gang who terrorized weaker kids at Moreville El? Good surveillance and undercover work nailed the planners of that horrible plot. It is all in the police report. The gang wanted revenge because Criss had successfully repelled previous attempts to get even by the younger gangsters at Moreville El. I'll get to those in order."

"Security had tightened up at Moreville El upon the advice of the police department, so it was impossible for the older gangsters to come on campus and do a quick hit-and-run on Criss using serious weaponry. This gang was driven to get Criss. They came up with a scheme to send five young gangsters, who were students enrolled at Moreville El, to shoot Criss. It was another failed plot, thank God. Criss wiped them all out as they ran out of a concealed closet."

More loud applause as Noe Itall sat motionless, seemingly resigned to the fact that this crowd was going to be heard. "The designated shooter was arrested with the intended murder weapon, a hot, small-caliber gun that was still in his pocket. He also had blood dripping from a self-inflicted gunshot wound, a wound that was meant for Criss. All of these misguided and unfortunate young boys are now in juvenile detention. I am sure you will agree that these were dangerous, young thugs. It just so happens that they were trying to earn acceptance into a smaller Mexican Mafia-type gang. They were not innocent students as the previous speaker claims. People everywhere have applauded Criss for his courage, just as you have here today."

"Let's go now to the incident preceding the attempted murder of Criss. Criss was running on the playground, as he frequently did, when eight or ten of his fellow students tried to 'get even' with Criss by forming two lines like a gauntlet. They hoped to lure the 'dim-witted' Criss to run through it as they inflicted as much punishment as possible. Criss wasn't dim-witted at all. In fact, he is quite the contrary. He sensed they were bad guys, so he proceeded to wipe the whole lot of them out single handedly. With blinding speed, he darted to one side throwing the gangsters off balance as he launched his little body and knocked them over like bowling pins."

More shouts of approval and applause erupted from the crowd that was now standing. "Ladies and gentlemen, boys and girls, you know these aggressors were not innocent students. They were little, would-be criminals in training."

"So, what was the genesis of all this gratuitous violence as the previous speaker might describe it? It happened to be that one of the gangsters at Moreville El was bigger and badder than any other kid on campus. A natural leader, but again not the innocent victim as the previous speaker claimed. No, Billy Benez would tell you himself, he was deserving of the beating that Criss gave him. Benez readily admits that he was accustomed to getting his way on campus. There were a lot of weaker kids with money in their pockets. It was easy until that day he got introduced to a new Criss with dynamite in his little body. Benez did spend some time in the hospital and then juvenile detention, but when he came out, he was eager to get back to Moreville El. Following his release, he came under the wing of a very special person." Pull finished by announcing, "Billy Benez is now doing very well as a foster son of Mrs. Mary Gonzales and her husband."

Mary came to the platform to say how happy she and her family were for the blessings Criss Crosswauld brought to her family. She then said, "As the reporters among you know, I have tried to shield Billy Benez from your inquiries about his take on the day that Criss Crosswauld confronted him. Billy is here beside me, and he wants to say something."

A hush fell over the noisy crowd. Everyone present knew about Billy. Billy haltingly took the microphone, "Um, I know what I want to say, but I don't know how to say it. I'm not a real good talker. Ah, when I saw Criss Cross on the playground that day, I thought he was just another easy mark. I grabbed the war medal he had in his pocket and um—um. As I stood there admiring the medal and trying to figure out if it was valuable, he suddenly came charging at me. Before I knew it, he was flying feet first like a torpedo launched right at me. I just stood there, scared as heck. I did not know what to do. I could not have escaped even if I had tried because his aim was good. As his body zoomed toward me, I knew I had been had. I felt a lot of heat from his feet, then I felt a thud, and then I sailed backwards landing flat on my back." Billy's facial expression seemed intense, and those in the front row swore they saw a trace of tears in his eyes as he continued. "Ah, I wanted to get up and run, but I couldn't. I could hardly move. For the first time in my life, I knew what it felt like to be helpless. I was sure he would stomp me and kick me until I begged for mercy. That is what I would have done to him. He didn't do that though. He just looked down at me and said something like 'get out.' It was as if he was talking to another person. Then he disappeared. I remember screaming and twitching all over. Then I passed out. I woke up in the hospital, not knowing if I was dead or alive. I tried to tell the people in the hospital how I felt, but they just said that I was OK and that I shouldn't get into fights. Over time, Mrs. Mary and her husband, Mr. Gonzales, have helped me to understand that Criss Cross did me a big favor. I lost all desire to take things that don't belong to me and to beat people up." He added with a huge smile, "Especially little guys with quick feet."

Mary took the microphone back as the crowd stood in shocked silence. She concluded by saying, "Billy is a changed human being. My husband, who as you know was a pretty good jock in his day, says he would not be surprised if that big body of Billy's finds its way onto the football field at DMU one day. But for now, all Billy wants is one of those T-shirts." With that the entire crowd jumped to their feet with applause and cheering, the likes of which was usually only seen when DMU scores the winning touchdown in a big game.

Pull, who was still sitting on the speaker's platform with Mary and Billy, feared the celebration might be premature because he saw what appeared to be a disturbance among the kids gathered in the front. A boy was shirtless and moving around rapidly, but he didn't hesitate to shout and applaud when he realized that the boy was Jack Crosswauld. Jack took off his T-shirt and handed it to Criss who immediately bounded up on the speaker's platform to give it to Billy. The surprised Billy grabbed the T-shirt, held it up for the crowd to see, and shouted, "Hey everybody, look at this!" Then he gave Criss a hearty high five which further energized the jubilant crowd. Whatever ill will there might have been melted like an ice cube in a frying pan.

The meeting was over. Noe Itall did not attempt to keep order. He had two choices: either slip away quietly with Hillary Cheatalot, Nancy P. Malaprop, and their few followers, or join the cheering crowd. Being a man with more political ambition than talent and integrity, he joined the winning side; slapping backs wildly and smiling as if he had been on Criss's side all along. He was even seen partaking in Pull's pizza and heard to say, "That Crosswauld kid is terrific. He personifies the high ideals I have worked so hard to instill in the students at Moreville El."

James B. (Bigbucks) Moore Jr. overhearing Noe Itall's comment turned to his ever-present administrative assistant—known as a bodyguard in other circles—and said with a grimace, "Did you hear that toad? Either he is the biggest liar in the country or he is delusional. Either way, it would be a disaster if he got his wish to be elected to high office."

"Yes sir," was the loud and clear response.

As things settled down, a fellow reporter who was tracking Hillary Cheatalot told Pull, "I could hardly believe my ears when I heard Cheatalot say, 'That stupid Benez kid just blew my case, and our chance to get some easy money. I don't know how many times I told him to keep his mouth shut.'"

To which Pull said, "Using the kid for her own gain, that fits the uber elitist mindset."

"What?" the reporter asked.

"Oh, never mind. Thanks for the input."

As the day drew to an end, Pull and Aggie—buoyed by the crowd's reaction, Billy Benez's comments, and a warm feeling of good will—had long since departed in Pull's dinky rental car for parts unknown; but not before commenting on the small group of well-dressed, Middle Eastern looking men in the back of the crowd.

Epilogue

The Crosswauld family goes on with a stressful life complicated by the very unusual situation of having the Agency monitor the family's affairs due to a perceived need to keep Uncle Jocko's death a secret. Criss's behavior continues to confound the family and experts alike, be they friend or foe. The delusional Ms. Hillary Cheatalot abandons all sense of civility in her grasp for power within an elitist-ruled world as she cultivates a closer relationship with Islamic terrorists. Pull Itzer decides he can pursue his blogging career in Moreville as well as anywhere and becomes a permanent resident. The Agency continues bureaucratically plodding to accomplish the purpose of its existence with full knowledge that the Crosswauld family is symbolic of the struggle mankind has confronted since the beginning of time. The Agency, keenly aware of history, knows that less than three hundred years have been free of organized conflict (war) during the past five millennia—three 'BCs' and two 'ADs'.[1]

Conflict has been an eternal plague of darkness that manifests itself in war and rumors of war. It will continue, as it is the human condition. The cause of goodness continues as well because it too is the human condition. The beat goes on until that time when the light will prevail, just as it has been written.

---

[1]   1. David G. Chandler, *The Time Chart History of War* (Ann Arbor, MI: Lowe & B. Howard, 2001) Page number 7